My Life Among the Aliens

My Life Among the Aliens

GAIL GAUTHIER

SCHOLASTIC INC.
New York Toronto London Auckland Sydney

For Will and Rob

Contents

1
How Mom
Saved the Planet

Aliens are around us all the time. Some of us can see them, some of us can't. It's just a matter of how you look at things and what you're looking for.

I first noticed aliens the morning Leo and Fred, two new kids from the end of our street, were supposed to come to our house for the day—and didn't. We hadn't met them yet, but our mother had met their mother.

I'm not an unfriendly person, but did Mom have to invite strange kids over on the first day of summer vacation? I don't think so. But that explains why we were expecting someone when the doorbell rang that morning. We were not, however, expecting what we got.

"Take us to your leader," an alien said as soon as Mom opened the door. There were two of them on our front step and they were both pointing awful-looking space weapons right at her.

"That's real cute, guys," Mom replied as she grabbed the death rays out of their hands, "but at this house we only play with Lego guns."

"Legos?" the spacemen said as they looked at each other.

"Are you by yourselves? Well, come on in. Will, show them where your toy box is," Mom told me. "Which one's Fred and which one's Leo?" she called over her shoulder as she ran back to the kitchen to make another phone call. She was trying to find someone to take care of Robby and me on Thursday afternoon so she could give a couple of music lessons at my father's music store. One of his regular teachers had broken his hand, which makes it real hard to play the guitar. Mom was going to fill in for him.

My father doesn't run one of those kinds of music stores that sells CDs and tapes. Oh, no. He says he's going to do that when he retires to Florida. Instead, he runs one of those kinds of music stores that sells and rents musical instruments and has rooms no bigger than closets where musicians—almost always adults—can give people—almost always kids—music lessons. I wish Dad would switch things around and sell electric guitars to old folks in Florida when he retires and sell CDs to kids now. I'd appreciate free CDs a whole lot more than I appreciate free music lessons.

Anyway, there I was, alone in my front hall with two aliens. And my mother had just told them that I still had a toy box.

You can imagine how I felt.

I did some quick thinking and took them to Robby's room and showed them *his* toy box. They started digging around in it right away. That left me free to run back to the kitchen, too.

"Mo-om," I said.

"Shh. I'm almost done," Mom replied as she started dialing another number.

"Mo-om," I said when she finally finished, "those guys are from outer space."

"They're from Orlando," she said. "Tell your brother to brush his teeth while I load the dishwasher. He's got a guest, so tell him not to dawdle."

Well, Mom didn't load the dishwasher because the telephone rang, and Robby didn't brush his teeth because I didn't tell him to.

I meant to tell him. I planned to. But when I got to his bedroom I found him showing one of the aliens how to play "Twinkle, Twinkle, Little Star" on his crummy little keyboard while the other one stretched out on his bed. (Did I mention that not only did Robby not brush his teeth that morning, he also didn't make his bed?)

"Twinkle, Twinkle, Little Star" was the only song

Robby could play back then, and he was pretty good at it. But the alien didn't seem to recognize it.

"Do you have any gum?" he asked.

"We're not allowed to chew gum," I explained.

The alien on the bed sat up suddenly. "No gum!" he shrieked.

"We're taking care of Brendan today!" Mom called, as she hung up the phone again. Brendan is our cousin. When he and Robby were babies, people used to call them the Twins because they were born just three weeks apart and all babies look alike. Their birthdays are still three weeks apart, of course, but they don't look alike anymore—not even close.

"Everybody get down to the car," Mom ordered. "We're going out for milk before he gets here."

We're always going out for milk.

I didn't want to sit next to the aliens, and Robby didn't want to sit next to me. Actually, the aliens didn't want to get into the car at all. Mom crammed us in where she wanted us and backed out of the garage. The alien she called Fred started to scream.

We invaded the grocery store. The aliens asked everyone in the aisles to take them to their leader. We ran into one of Mom's friends, who wanted to know if the guitar quartet Mom and Dad belong to could perform at her niece's wedding; one of my friends, who wanted to know if I could come over later in the week; and one of Robby's friends, who told him that a girl neither one of them liked was going to be in their swimming class. I'm sure I saw one of Mom's private guitar students, one of the ones who won't practice, but she saw us coming and ran out of the store.

I guess you could say it was a productive trip for the human members of our party, what with Mom getting a job, me getting an invitation, and Rob getting bad news. Leo and Fred, however, got nothing. No one would take them anywhere.

"We want Legos," Leo or Fred said as soon as we got home.

"Great. You can play with Legos while Will and Robby pick up their rooms. Then they'll play with you."

Sure, I thought.

The next time I saw them, Leo and Fred had turned on the television. They were pointing Lego guns at Bert and Ernie and saying, "Take us to your leader."

"You guys are a hoot," Mom laughed, as she came into the living room with the vacuum cleaner. "But we don't watch television here until after lunch." She snapped off the TV. "You can watch it this afternoon."

Leo turned his weapon on her, but she didn't notice because she was plugging in the vacuum cleaner. Then he tried to evaporate *that*, and Fred covered his ears and screamed. A lot of good that did him. My mother doesn't stop vacuuming for mere screaming. She's really proud of how fast she can vacuum a room, and she says the secret is to not stop for *anything*. If you're fast enough, she says, nothing can happen that's so bad it can't wait until you're done.

Rob and I gave up screaming while Mom vacuumed *ages* ago.

Fred had a good pair of lungs—or a good pair of whatever it is that makes aliens scream loudly. I think it may have been a little while before I noticed our doorbell ringing and let my cousin Brendan in.

"Aunt Connie! Aunt Connie!" I shouted to his mother. "We've got aliens here today!"

"Good for you!" Aunt Connie shouted back. "Gotta run. Have a good time."

I grabbed Brendan's arm and pointed to Leo and Fred, who were trying to get their deathray guns off the top of the refrigerator while Mom whipped through the dining room. "Those guys over there are spacemen," I said.

Brendan said, "Cool."

"You can have your toys back when you go home," Mom said when she got to the kitchen. Then she gave Brendan a kiss and told us we had to go outside and play.

We all went outdoors, where Leo fell off my bike, and Fred cried. We couldn't make them understand how to play hide-and-seek, and Fred cried. They could run but not very fast, so we played *a lot* of tag. And Fred cried.

Tommy O. came over from next door. Fred asked him to take him to his leader. Leo said, "We are here to take over your planet."

"Why?" Tommy asked.

That's why Tommy is my best friend. I like a guy who doesn't panic.

Robby made us look at his acorn collection. Brendan

liked it because he likes everything Robby does, but Leo and Fred said they had a better one at home.

Like I'm supposed to believe they have acorns on other planets.

We ate lunch out on the deck. Brendan didn't like the mustard I put on his hot dog, and Mom made me take it in and wash it off. Fred had trouble figuring out how to eat a hot dog and roll at the same time. Tommy ate two of each before Mom had a chance to call his mother to see if he could stay for lunch.

"You call this food?" Leo asked.

"It's the best you can hope for at this house," I explained. "It wouldn't even be this good if we didn't have company."

Leo refused to touch anything on his plate, but Fred sucked up everything Mom would give him. I had to be careful to hold on to anything I wanted.

"Are you ready for dessert?" Mom asked.

"What is it? Cookies? Cake? Ice cream?" I knew it wasn't any of that stuff, but I like to pretend.

"Is it gum?" Fred asked hopefully.

"Bran muffins," Mom answered as she passed them out.

Well, Leo did like bran muffins. He and Fred liked *all* of them.

"How are things going?" Mom asked as I helped her bring dirty dishes into the kitchen.

"They really are from outer space, Mom. They want to take over our planet."

Mom laughed and kissed me on the forehead. "Have a good time," she said.

Have a good time? With the fate of the world resting on my shoulders?

The first thing we had to do, I figured, was distract Leo and Fred so the rest of us could get together and make a plan. When Tommy said he wanted to play Capture the Flag, I saw my chance. While Robby took Leo and Fred into the house to look for a couple of my father's old shirts to use for flags, I pulled Tommy and Brendan aside and told them that I thought we'd better do something about the alien situation.

"Why?" Tom asked.

"You've heard them. They want to take over our planet."

"Maybe we should tell Aunt Reggie," Brendan suggested.

"I have told her. You know what she said? She said, 'Have a good time.' We are the Earth's only hope."

Brendan and Tommy agreed that that was pretty neat.

"We've got to show them that humans are tough," I explained. "We've got to scare them so badly they give up their plan for world domination."

Tom thought he could do that.

"There are four of us and only two of them," Brendan pointed out. "The odds are in our favor."

When Leo and Fred came back, we explained the rules for Capture the Flag and told them that the two of them would be on one team and the four of us would be on another.

"Well, that's not fair," Robby started to say. "Why don't you . . ."

"This is an alien versus human game," I explained. I looked at Leo and Fred. "You guys don't have a problem with that, do you?"

They looked at each other and nodded their heads. "There are four of you and two of us," Leo said. "The odds are clearly in our favor."

"Hey," Tommy called to me as we took off to hide Dad's Hard Rock Cafe T-shirt, "I thought the odds were supposed to be in *our* favor?"

They *were* in our favor. And they got better, because Tommy's little sister, Katie, came over with one of her friends to join the game. Then a couple of guys we know were riding by on their bikes so they stopped by. A friend of Tommy's drove by with his mother. She stopped and let him out so he could play, too. That meant there were nine of us playing against the two aliens.

We had three experienced people guarding our flag. Katie and Robby created a diversion by pretending to kill each other at the very edge of the enemy territory while our fastest players risked being tagged so they could seek out and capture the alien flag. We even had spies. We had it all.

Leo and Fred took our flag three times. They also ended up with Katie's headband, some hard candies

Robby had been keeping in his pocket, and one of Tommy's socks.

"You shouldn't have been able to do that. You were outnumbered," Brendan insisted. His glasses kept flowing down his nose on streams of sweat. "It shouldn't have happened."

Leo turned to Fred and laughed. "And you were worried about coming here!"

Tommy's face was so red he looked as if he was going to pop. "They must have some kind of secret weapon. That's the only explanation."

"Do you want to play again?" Leo asked. He didn't sound as if he was interested in a friendly game.

We lost two more times before we began to lose interest in saving the world. People started drifting off. When Mom asked if we wanted anything to eat there was just six of us again—two aliens and their four future slaves. She took us inside and made us some popcorn, which Leo and Fred used for bombs.

"We don't do that here," Mom said sternly.

"It is a custom in our homeland," Leo replied.

"This *is* our homeland," Mom told him.

Leo shot a popcorn at Fred.

"Mom, maybe you shouldn't make these guys mad," I warned. "Do you know how many times they beat us at Capture the Flag?"

I guess Leo was the one who shouldn't have made Mom mad. She made Leo sit in the bathroom for five minutes. Fred screamed and Leo kicked the door, but that kind of thing never bothers Mom. Leo was not a happy spaceman when he came out.

He perked up when we went back outside. Fred wanted to try the swing, but Leo wanted to escape. He said he was going to ask the neighbors to take him to their leader.

He was asking for trouble. And when Mom looked out the front window and saw him walking up the street, he got it.

"Get into this house, Leo!"

Leo started to run.

She caught him just as she's caught every kid who ever tried to leave our yard by themselves. No one gets away from Mom.

He was still sitting on our couch with his hands in his lap when we went back into the house.

"Tommy's mom said he had to go home," Robby explained. "Let's watch TV."

"There is more than one mom?" Leo asked. He seemed kind of surprised.

"Sure," I answered. "Everyone has one."

"How many is everyone?" Leo wanted to know.

"Millions and billions," Brendan replied.

Fred began to cry.

"Do they all run around giving orders all the time?" Leo asked.

Robby answered him. "All the ones I know do."

I was beginning to get an idea. "Moms make you take baths, and they wash your hair. They make you change your underwear every day. They won't let you play in the street, and they tell you to go to bed when they know you're not tired."

"But they read to you," Robby broke in. "And they take you places and buy you things . . ."

"Except for gum!" I broke in. "They never buy you gum!"

"Millions and billions of moms?" Leo repeated.

"We'll be lucky if we get away," Fred sobbed.

"I like moms," Robby said. "They invite me to their houses and . . ."

I quickly interrupted him. "They won't let you wear your favorite clothes to school because they have holes in them or they're dirty. When you go to the lake, they won't let you go in water over your head. They make you take music lessons and do your homework. And, remember, they won't let you have gum."

"So moms run everything here?" Leo asked.

"On this planet, you can't do anything unless a mom says you can."

Fred sniffed. "We've made a terrible mistake."

"If you think my mother is bad," I whispered, "you ought to meet my grandmothers."

"We've got two of those," Robby said.

Leo jumped off the couch. "Get our firearms. We're going home."

When Mom came into the living room, Robby, Brendan, and I were watching "Star Trek."

"Where are Leo and Fred?" she asked.

"They went home," I told her.

"By themselves? Did their mother come get them? I didn't hear the doorbell ring."

"She didn't ring the doorbell."

"Why didn't she come in and tell me she was taking them? She must be a very strange woman."

Well, I thought, she'd have to be, wouldn't she?

2
The Interstellar Games

After that first visit I figured, what were the chances of aliens coming to my house again? I know Earth isn't the biggest planet in the solar system, but still there must be lots of places aliens could go here without coming to my street *twice*. So I wasn't paying much attention. Maybe if I had been I would have noticed something sooner. Or maybe the next alien only came by because it was my birthday.

And not just any birthday. It was my ninth birthday.

My ninth birthday, which just happened to fall during an Olympic year.

Thank goodness that won't be happening again.

My brother and I aren't allowed to have birthday parties at restaurants or bowling alleys or public pools like our friends do. My mother says those kinds of parties aren't challenging enough. My mother says paying someone to entertain and feed a group of children shows a lack of creativity. My mother says any mom who won't make her kid a birthday cake or party invitations is a wimp.

My father says to stay out of Mom's way when she's planning a party. He says no one is safe while she's making favors. He says no force on Earth can stop her.

For my ninth birthday my mother planned an Olympic Games just for me. I don't know anyone else who's had one. Dad says that if I'm lucky, I'll never have another. Mom spent a month getting ready for that party. All my friends came.

And then some.

The Opening Ceremonies were scheduled for four o'-clock on a Sunday afternoon. My cousin Brendan came the night before and Tommy and Katie O. arrived early because they live right next door. Then Ian, Jonathan, Ryan, and Jason came. If you add my brother Robby and me you get nine kids.

''. . . six, seven, eight, nine, ten . . . Something's wrong here. I only planned for nine children. Did I forget someone?'' Mom asked.

Mom often forgets someone.

"Oh, no," Dad groaned.

". . . Brendan, Robby, and Will. I'm sure we didn't invite anyone else. But who's that tall boy . . . girl . . . child . . . over there?" Mom asked me.

I looked over toward the deck, where my presents were stacked on a little round table. There was an uninvited guest there, all right. He . . . she . . . it . . . was wearing something all in one piece with long sleeves and long legs. It didn't have a belt, and there was extra material under the arms that made this big kid look sort of like a flying squirrel.

It wasn't what I would have chosen to wear to a birthday party in August.

"Hey, Will, who's that?" Robby asked me.

I shrugged.

"I'll find out," he offered.

"No! It's my party. I'll find out who he . . . it is."

Robby doesn't listen to a word I say. He was already tearing over to the table.

"What are you doing here?" Robby asked.

"I am here to learn how to make friends. Do you know how to do that?"

"Sure," Robby answered.

"Good. How do you make friends?"

"Ah . . ."

"What about you? Do you know?"

"I just go up and start talking to people," I explained.

"Fine. I'm talking to you, so you are my friend."

"I . . . I guess so."

"Are you a boy or a girl?" Robby asked.

"Am I supposed to be a boy or a girl?"

"Everybody is either a boy or a girl."

"How do I know which I am?"

Robby and I looked at each other. "Looks like we've got another alien situation here," I told him. I *was* kind of surprised. But, still, I know an alien when I see one. So does Robby.

He turned around and started running and shouting for Mom.

"It's my party!" I yelled as I ran after him. "I want to tell her!"

". . . another alien," Robby was saying when I caught up to him.

"Don't listen to him, Mom. Let me tell you," I cried.

"What? What? What? Tell me what?"

"That strange kid over there? He's an alien."

Mom shook her head at me. "Will, did you invite someone without asking me first? You know you're not supposed to do that."

"How could I invite an alien? Where would I send the invitation?"

"Call the police, Mom. Or the FBI. Or the army. You gotta call somebody," Robby insisted.

"This is going to ruin my party!"

"That's hardly a reason to call the police," Mom pointed out.

"Have these boys been watching 'The X-Files,'

Regina?'' Dad asked. Dad always calls Mom Regina whenever he thinks he has something important to say. ''They wouldn't be like this if they watched 'Sesame Street.' There are no strange creatures on that show.''

Obviously, Dad doesn't watch much television.

''Calm down, everybody, just calm down.'' I'm not sure if Mom was talking to us or to two kids who were having a fight. ''I don't know how this happened, but . . . she's just a child. We can't just send her away. It would hurt her feelings.''

''He's a space guy,'' I reminded her. ''He may not have feelings.''

''Now, RJ,'' Mom said to my father, ''after the Opening Ceremonies, go up to the street and take a look around. Someone may be looking for this girl. If you can't find anyone, go into the house and make up another goody bag. There's some extra candy in the cupboard over the refrigerator, and you'll find some small toys in that box in my closet.''

''Why do I have to do it?'' Dad asked.

''Oh, you don't, dear. You can stay out here with these ten children and run this party while I go in the house and take care of it,'' Mom offered.

''No more birthdays!'' Dad roared. ''These kids are staying nine and seven for the rest of their lives!''

''Good plan, RJ,'' Mom said as she headed over to the alien.

''What's your name, dear?'' she asked.

"Phlip."

"Philippa? I like that. You don't hear that often."

I wonder why, I thought.

"Well, Philippa," Mom said, "this is Will and his brother Robby. And I'm Will's mom. Did your mother or father drop you off?"

"Yes. That's exactly what happened. My mother or father dropped me."

"What? . . . Hey! Who's fighting over there! . . . Well, we'd better get this thing going. Let the Games begin!" Mom shouted over the screaming.

Dad played the Olympic theme music. It sounded really good even though he hadn't been able to find sheet music for it. Mom had wanted the other members of their guitar quartet to play at my party, too. But one of them thought he was too old to learn something as difficult as the Olympic theme, and the other said Dad couldn't pay him enough to play at a kid's party. So Dad got out his old electric guitar and some speakers. He did a great job. All the neighbors said so.

Mom had made each of the partygoers a flag of a foreign country. They were tacked to sticks, and we were supposed to carry them up over our heads while we ran. But they made such good swords and Ninja Turtle sticks that most of us didn't bother. Phlip didn't have a flag, of course. There was no telling what place he represented. He wasn't much of a runner, either, but he sure could scream and shout.

We ran around the house three times. Then my mother decided she'd had enough of that, so she said it was time for the first event. Then she said it again. And again.

The first event was a race. We were supposed to run two kids at a time, with the winners running against each other. It was kind of complicated, so we just all ran across the backyard.

The second event was a race, too. We were supposed to run a relay race. That was really complicated, so we all just ran across the backyard.

The third event was a long jump. We were supposed to lay two brooms down on the ground and jump from one to the other. That was so complicated that we just gave up and stomped on all the balloons Mom and Dad had blown up the night before.

"How's it going, Reggie?" Dad asked Mom when he came out of the house with a plastic bag with a chain saw printed on the outside of it.

"We're moving right along. You didn't find any stray parents out in the street?"

"I didn't find any parents of any sort out there. If no one turns up to claim him, we'll . . ."

"Is that the best thing you could find for a goody bag?" Mom broke in.

"Yes, it is," Dad snapped. "And I couldn't find the box of toys in your closet so I had to come up with something myself."

Mom grabbed the bag out of his hands and looked in it. "Socks? You're giving her socks?"

"They're brand new, never been worn, *and* they're athletic socks so they fit in with the sports theme for this party." Dad sounded real proud of himself.

"Let's see what else you've got here . . . pencils with your music store's name engraved on them . . . a notepad from the store . . . three guitar picks stamped with the store's name . . . and an address book." She shook her head in disgust. "This is the kind of stuff kids *love* to get for party favors."

"I'*d* be happy to get it," Dad said defensively.

Mom brought out a giant watermelon then, because the seed-spitting event was next.

While we were waiting for our watermelon, Phlip said, "Mom said you and Robby are siblings. How can that be?"

"Your mother told you that? Do we know your mother?"

"No, Mom—that short, bossy woman over there. She said you were brothers. How can that be?"

"We have the same mother and father," I explained.

"But if you are both products of the same genetic pool, members of the same litter, brothers, how come you don't look alike?"

"We look a lot alike," I said. And we do.

"But you're taller than your brother. You have blond hair and green eyes, and he has brown hair and brown eyes."

"Well, except for *all that* we look a lot alike. Do your brothers and sisters look a lot alike?"

"*Exactly* alike."

We had tried and tried to explain racing to Phlip, but

he just didn't understand. We didn't have to tell him twice how to spit watermelon seeds, though. Obviously, he had done it before. Tommy O. is the best seed spitter on our street, and he couldn't even come close to Phlip. After a while, we all gave up trying. We gave Phlip all our seeds, set up targets for him, and told him to let 'er rip. He hit everything. If a target was too far away, he'd spit while running toward it. He could spit over his shoulder and still hit his mark.

We would have been happy to watch Phlip spit for the rest of the afternoon, but he accidentally broke my cousin's glasses. It was a good thing he was wearing them, because otherwise Phlip would have put out Brendan's eye with that seed.

"This is how Phlip's people take over other planets," Robby whispered to me. "They spit bullets and bombs and junk like that. It is so . . . gross!"

"Time for the dance contest!" Mom called.

"I guess I'd better go get the pizza," Dad said as he slunk off toward the driveway.

"Come back here, you coward!" Mom shouted after him.

"Oh, Reggie! Don't make me!"

She made him.

"I've got your favorite dance music, RJ."

"There's no such thing as good dance music," Dad said as Mom pulled the tape player out from under a chair, turned it on, and stood in front of him. She took each of his hands in hers and started jitterbugging. He waited patiently for her to finish.

She rewound the tape and announced that was just a warm-up, now we were *really* going to dance.

"Hey, what happened to my dance partner?" Mom asked after she had everything all ready to go again.

We all laughed and pointed to the driveway. Dad's car was pulling out onto the street.

"Well, I'll take care of him when he gets back with the pizza. In the meantime, I guess I'll just have to find someone else to dance with me, won't I?" she said. Then she did a witch's laugh (which she does *awfully* well) and started wringing her hands together as she looked us all over. We all screamed and ran and hid behind trees and each other.

"I'll dance with you, Mom!"

Phlip grabbed Mom around the waist with one arm, took her free hand with his other, and they were off!

Well, we'd never seen Mom dance with anyone near her own height. Dad's a lot taller than she is. Heck, we'd never seen Mom dance with anyone who would dance back. Dad stands so still Mom calls him her May Pole. So you can understand that even if Mom hadn't been dancing with an alien, we would have been kind of surprised.

We were—all of us—speechless.

"Spit and dance—that must be all they do on his planet," said Robby. "Gee, do you suppose if I practiced I could spit as good as he does someday?"

"Well, thank you, Philippa," Mom said after the song

was over. "It's been a long time since I danced with someone who knew how. I'm not sure I like it."

The last sporting event of the day was Statue. We had to see who could hold still and be silent the longest.

We were through with that before Mom got the juice poured for dinner.

We were too excited to eat much (which turned out pretty good for Robby and me—we got to eat leftover pizza for breakfast, lunch, AND dinner the next day). Dad doesn't like Mom to sing in front of us because he's afraid it will stunt our growth, so he kept his hand over her mouth while my friends sang Happy Birthday. My cake was made out of five round cakes scrunched together and decorated to look like the Olympic rings. Nobody could figure out what it was, though everyone thought it was neat that there was so much of it. (There was a lot of that left over, too.)

Then came the part of the party that *everyone* was waiting for—watching me, the birthday boy, open my presents. I got a baseball glove that is now too small for me, a space coloring book that I let somebody borrow and never saw again, a bike horn that I never got a chance to use, a lunch box with a Thermos bottle that leaked, a decorate-your-own T-shirt that I never did and now it doesn't fit anymore, a bug net that my mother sat on so the handle is bent, and school clothes from Brendan's mother.

It's hard to feel thankful when you're holding a geeky green turtleneck sweater, but I managed to thank everybody anyway.

"So this party is over?" Phlip asked.

Dad answered him. "I sure hope so."

Phlip turned and started to walk away.

"Are you leaving, Phillipa?" Mom asked. "Wait just a moment. I have a little present for you."

Phlip came back onto the deck. "How nice," he said. "I'll take this."

And he snatched my brand-new bicycle horn off my stack of presents and left.

"Mom!" I howled. "Dad! He's leaving with my horn!"

"But he *is* leaving!" Dad hissed. "Let him go!"

Then he handed me that crummy chain saw bag with the socks that were mine to begin with.

" 'H*e* is leaving'?" Mom repeated. "He's not a he, he's a she."

Mom ran around to the front of the house because she has this big thing about kids not wandering around loose by themselves. But Phlip was already gone.

"Where could she have gone?" Mom wondered.

Well, there *are* eight other planets in this solar system.

"Hey!" Robby exclaimed. "There's a box under the table." He dove right under there to get it.

"Who's this from?" I asked.

Nobody answered so I thought, Great, this must be underwear from my mother or sheets or something like that. But when I opened the box I found one of those red-and-blue balls with stripes and stars like little kids play with.

"That's a baby present!" Robby said.

Mom just looked at him.

"It's a very, very *nice* baby present," he added.

I had a lot of trouble getting the ball out of the box because whenever my hand got close to it, the ball would move. I finally just turned the box upside down and let the ball drop onto the deck. It bounced and rolled and somebody tried to pick it up and it rolled some more. Then someone else tried to pick it up, and it rolled another way.

We played with that ball for the next twenty minutes. My friends' parents had to drag them out of the yard and down the street because they didn't want to leave. Robby and I played with it until it got dark, then we got flashlights and played some more. I couldn't pick the ball up to take care of it, so I had to chase it into the house when we went in for the night. Then I had to chase it down the hall to my bedroom.

The Ball was our favorite toy for the rest of the summer. We'd run outside in our pajamas before breakfast to play with it. We didn't watch TV after dinner because we had to go out and play with The Ball. Friends dropped by almost every day to see what was happening with The Ball. Big kids we hardly knew pulled into our driveway with their bicycles so they could check out The Ball. *Moms* came to see The Ball.

Whatever it was, it was the best I've ever had.

Unfortunately, I lost it.

3
Man's Best Friend Could Be an Alien

I was glad that not every alien who comes here wants to stake a claim to our world. But there was a part of me that was a little offended, too. I mean, who wants to live on a planet no one else wants? You have to wonder about the judgment of some of these aliens.

Now, Robby and I knew we had been visited by aliens twice. And, yes, we knew that was weird. What we didn't know was just how weird things were going to get.

And then Dad caught the Keiths' dog digging a hole in our garden. . . .

"What's that mutt's name? Judy?" he asked that night at supper.

"That's my mother's name," Mom complained. "The dog's name is Sandy."

Dad gave me a little kick under the table. "I bet a lot of people make that mistake, huh?"

"She knocked down my fort and got into the O.'s garbage," Robby announced.

I gave Dad a little kick under the table. "Grandma?" I asked.

"No! Sandy!"

"She tore Mrs. Paige's laundry off her clothesline and chased cars for half an hour," Mom told us.

And I was able to add that Mr. Keith, who lived just the other side of our driveway, had told me that he didn't know how she did it, but she'd found a way to get off her leash so many times that he'd given up putting it on her. Sandy, I mean, not Grandma.

"She was a perfect dog until yesterday afternoon," Mom said. "I just don't understand it. She was better trained than most of the kids on this street."

She frowned at us as she said that.

"Well, Mom, *we've* never knocked over other people's garbage or torn their wet stuff off their clothesline. At least, I haven't. Maybe Robby has."

"I have not! Will chases cars, though, Mom. I've seen him."

Mom said it was time to take our dishes out to the

kitchen. Then she told our father that she thought Sandy had gone bad because of our poor influence.

We get blamed for everything around here.

"Can that happen?" Robby asked me. "Could Sandy have started doing bad things because of us?"

"Of course not," I told him. "We don't chase cars—neither one of us."

"Why do dogs do that?" he wondered. "It's dangerous, and they get punished for it. Besides, what would they do with a car if they caught it? Bury it?"

I thought that was a pretty good one—bury a car!

The next afternoon when Robby and I got off the bus we noticed Sandy walking down the street. She noticed us, too, and started racing right toward us. Now, we've been told over and over again never to run from an excited dog because it will think we want to play and chase us. We've been told never to scream and shout around a dog because that will scare it, and dogs do ugly things when they're scared. We've been told never to hurt a dog.

But we were never told what to do if a full-grown golden retriever came for us, barking what sounded an awful lot like "Lunch!"

We were totally on our own.

Robby dropped his school bag. I was wearing a backpack, and I couldn't get it off. That's the only reason Robby was able to get ahead of me going down our driveway. Otherwise I would have beaten him. I don't know where I would have gone if I'd made it down the driveway first, but I certainly wouldn't have gone up that flowering dogwood the way Robby did.

It makes Mom real mad when he does that.

Remember, I still had my backpack on. It's hard to climb any tree with a backpack on, but it's especially hard to shinny up one of those skinny dogwoods. I did darn good to get as far off the ground as I did. And I went far enough. I could feel Sandy's breath on my ankles, but not her teeth. Sure, Robby went a whole lot higher. But he was just showing off.

Sandy threw herself down on the ground, rolled onto her back, and exclaimed, "Oh, what a glorious afternoon!"

"No, it's not a glorious afternoon!" Robby shouted from over my head. "I lost a library book, and I got in trouble in school because Greg Hooper was talking and Ms. D. thought it was me!"

"Robby! You're talking to a dog!" I said to him.

"Oops!" Sandy jumped onto her feet and started for the Keiths' yard. "Just forget you heard that."

Yeah. Like I'm going to forget that a dog just spoke to me.

Robby made it to the ground first because he swung down from a tiny little branch and dropped a couple of feet. We're not supposed to do that. I got down the way we're supposed to.

"Come on," I said as I finally got that backpack off. "We're going after that dog."

When we got around the picket fence that separates our yard from the Keiths', we found Sandy lying in front of her doghouse. She had her eyes closed. We stood over her and watched for a while.

"She's only pretending to be asleep," I told Robby.

Robby thought so, too. "Nobody pants like that while they're sleeping. Not even dogs."

We both screeched and jumped back as Sandy leaped to her feet, looked both ways, and started running into the woods behind our houses. There's a lot of brush back there *and* dead leaves *and* rocks. It's easy to slip and fall even when it's not wet. We both ended up on our backsides two or three times, I landed on my hands once, which really hurt, and Robby caught a branch across his face, which made him yell something fierce, so I guess that hurt, too.

It's funny, though, how little those kinds of things bother you when you're trying to catch a talking dog.

We could see Sandy way down by the creek in back of our house.

"Go back and ask Mom if we can go down to the creek," I said.

"Sandy might be gone by the time I get back. This is important. Mom will understand if we go down to the creek without asking."

I reminded Robby about what Mom said would happen the next time we went to the creek without telling her. He ran back up the hill to our house.

Well, I lost sight of Sandy for a while. One minute she

was walking along the creek, the next minute she was gone. And the next minute . . .

The next minute she was after me again.

I just made it to our giant rocks. I scrambled up the lower ones with her just behind me. I thought dogs couldn't climb rocks. They can—not very well, but you don't have to be good at it to get up them. I was at the top of the biggest rock with a drop-off behind me. Sandy was sort of stretched out in front of me—she had her back legs on a lower rock and her front legs on the rock I was curled up on. She barked at me a few times. Then she whimpered and whined. She kept looking at me and then looking over her shoulder.

I sat there just as quietly as I could. Not that I had any choice. There was no place I could go, there was nothing I could do. That's not right. I could think. I could think things like "Do talking dogs bite the way regular ones do?" and "Do the Keiths feed Sandy before they go to work in the morning or after they get home in the afternoon?"

Suddenly Sandy gave one loud bark—a very happy-sounding bark—and jumped down from the rocks. I watched her head back up the hill, right toward Robby, who was coming down it.

"Run, Rob!" I screamed. "Run for your life!"

Robby saw Sandy coming for him and didn't need to ask any questions. He took off up the hill, Sandy followed him; I got down off the rocks and followed her.

We shot out of the woods and across our back lawn. Mom was just carrying a load of clean wash in from the clothesline.

"Stay away from the road!" she called. "If you want something to eat, come get it soon. I have a guitar student arriving at three-thirty."

Between our house and our neighbors', the O.'s, is a piece of land where the boundary between our property is supposed to be. Everyone knows it's there, but no one knows exactly where *there* is. So nobody knows who is supposed to be responsible for what. It's a No Mom's Land. No Mom mows the lawn out there. No Mom rakes the leaves. When we're playing in No Mom's Land, no Mom watches us. If we leave our stuff there, no Mom picks it up. If we fight, no Mom will break us up unless she hears the word *blood*, and then there'd better be plenty of it when she arrives at the scene.

Robby led us across our backyard to our driveway, over that to the pine trees at the front of our front lawn, among those, across the clearing where we slide in the winter, into No Mom's Land. He jumped over what was left of the fort Sandy had wrecked the day before and stopped on top of the flat rock where we have picnics.

"Don't move!" I shouted to Robby. "Hold perfectly still."

Sandy spun around and looked at me. I stopped in my tracks and didn't move. She looked from one of us to the other. She jumped at me. I gritted my teeth and stood my ground. She leaped up onto the rock with Robby. He didn't even look down at her.

She marched halfway between us and said, "Run for me, humans."

"There! There! Did you hear that! She talked again!" Robby yelled.

"I order you to run for me," Sandy said.

"Who died and left you boss?" I asked.

"Well, I *am* a member of the dominant species on this planet," she replied.

"The what?" Robby asked.

I wasn't sure what she was talking about, either, but I would never have let a dog know that.

"I am a dog," Sandy explained. "You are human boys. You run for me, you throw sticks for me, you take me for walks. Now get started."

"Have you always been able to talk?" I wanted to know.

"Of course."

"Then how come you never have?"

"I've been talking all my life, I'll have you know. I have talked with some of the greatest talkers of my world. We have talked at great length about a great many things."

"Ah," I said. "You're an alien, aren't you?"

"No, no, no," she said very quickly—a little *too* quickly, if you know what I mean. "I am *not* an alien. I am a dog."

Robby jumped off the rock and stood in front of Sandy. "You're not the real Sandy, are you?" he said in a real mean voice. "What have you done with her? Did you hide her somewhere? Did you send her to the pound? You didn't . . . you didn't kill her, did you?"

"Of course not. I would never harm such an intelligent, sensitive creature. Your Sandy is perfectly safe. We have merely traded places. Right this moment she is giving a lecture to the Academy of Intergalactic Life Sciences on the nutritional needs of Earth life-forms."

Robby made a face. "What do you suppose she's saying?"

"So you admit you're not Sandy. Then who are you?" I demanded.

"A researcher. A scientist. A student. Someone who has done nothing, nothing I tell you, but work all her life. I have to say, I am having one good time on this planet."

She picked up a stick in her mouth and handed it to me. "Throw it," she ordered.

"Again," she said when she brought the stick back to me.

"Again," she repeated after she brought it back a second time.

By then I figured I had enough dog spit on me, and I refused to throw it anymore.

"All right. Then take me for a walk."

"You've just been all over our yard. What do you want to go for a walk for?" Robby asked.

"I am a dog. I have a right to expect humans to take me for a walk."

"Ask one of the Keiths to take you. You're their dog."

"Robby, could you come over here for a minute?" I

pulled him away from the dog and whispered, "This is an alien who was able to get here from another planet and switch places with a dog without anyone knowing about it. Do you really want to get in a fight with her?"

"No. But I don't want to take her for a walk, either."

"We have to be very careful about what we do here," I warned him.

"Okay, I'll be careful," Robby agreed. "But I'm *not* taking her for a walk."

"Do you have a name?" I asked the dog after I'd finished with Robby.

"You may continue to call me Sandy."

"I feel kind of funny about doing that since you're not the real Sandy. Then when the real Sandy comes back, it will be confusing to have to start calling her Sandy again. What were you called on your planet?"

"It doesn't matter. I'm Sandy now."

"And just what planet are you from?" Robby asked.

"You two haven't been there." Sandy laughed. It was a strange sound that would have been easy to mistake for a growl, except she was smiling. "You wouldn't know it."

Personally, I think she came from that Dog Star—Sirius or whatever it is. It makes sense.

"How long did it take you to get here?" I asked.

"How long are you staying?" Robby wanted to know.

"Do you talk to anyone else?"

"To other dogs?"

"How do you keep getting off your leash?"

"Why do you chase cars?"

"Humans! You question everything! That's the reason no other species in the universe will have anything to do with you." Sandy started walking back toward the Keiths' yard and her doghouse.

"How many species are there in the universe?" I shouted after her.

We told Mom and Dad about Sandy talking and being an alien and all. Dad was in a hurry because he was going to perform with some singer at eight. He said that if Sandy was talking to stay away from her. A dog that talked was no good to anybody.

We took Mom over to the Keiths' after supper, and we all stood around looking at Sandy, who was stretched out on the chaise on Mrs. Keith's deck.

"Okay, go on. Say something," Robby told her.

Sandy opened one eye, then closed it.

"Tell us how you got here. Do you have a spaceship hidden someplace or is it circling the planet waiting for you?" I asked.

"Ask her what kinds of bones she likes best," Mom suggested.

I offered to buy her a pretty rubber ball if she spoke.

"Look! Look!" Robby exclaimed. "See how she twitched when Will said he'd buy her a ball?"

"Face it, guys, she's not going to talk—at least not in front of me." Mom rubbed behind Sandy's ears and said, "What's this? No flea collar? And look at the burrs. You're not taking very good care of yourself, are you, old girl?"

Then Mom rapped on the glass door that led into the Keiths' family room. They let her in, and we could hear her laughing and talking in there with Mr. and Mrs. Keith.

Sandy got up and jumped off the chaise. "Old girl? Old girl? She has her nerve calling me an old girl."

"Well, you are old," I told her. "Or Sandy is. Robby's seven, and she's older than he is. That's old for a dog."

"She's very fortunate I showed up, then. I can make this body last a good long time, and she is much better off in the one she has now."

"What do you mean you can make it last a long time? Are you planning to stay a long time?" I asked.

We had followed the dog back to her house. She took a drink out of her bowl, then said, "Only if you consider the rest of my life a long time."

"You want to spend the rest of your life as a dog?" Robby asked in amazement.

Sandy turned on him. "Why not?" she asked. "Dogs have wonderful lives. Someone brings them their food, someone brings them their water. They're provided with housing. They do nothing but play, eat, and sleep."

"Some dogs have to work," I broke in.

"I haven't met any," Sandy said. "This is a whole lot better life than the one I had, and I'm keeping it."

"What about the real Sandy?" I complained.

"What about her?"

"Maybe she doesn't like the life she has now. Maybe she'd rather be what she was supposed to be—a dog."

"What is she now, anyway?" Robby asked.

"She is me. Or she is what I was."

"And you didn't like that," I pointed out. "Why should she?"

"I lived that life for years and years!" Sandy shouted. "It's someone else's turn now. I've got a chance at a great life, and I'm going to take it. No one can blame me. I don't know anyone who wouldn't jump at the chance to live a dog's life."

"What are you doing here, anyway?" Robby asked. "Why did you come to this planet?"

"I came to study life on Earth. And now I've decided I like it here, and I'm going to stay. It happens all the time."

"What?" I exclaimed. "You mean there are other aliens here? Aliens who came to study us and decided to stay?"

Sandy gave that rough laugh of hers again. "Look around."

"Guys! Let's get headed home!"

The sound of Sandy's laugh followed us past the picket fence as we followed our mother back to our house.

"Mom!" I said. "She's not going to let the real Sandy come back. She wants to keep Sandy's body for herself. That's not right."

Mom laughed. "If I were an alien, I wouldn't want Sandy's body."

"What do you mean?" I asked.

"As luck would have it, Sandy has an appointment tomorrow with the veterinarian. She needs a little work done on her fleas, she needs to have her nails trimmed . . . let's see, what else did Mrs. Keith say? Oh, yes. She's going to have her teeth cleaned, and it's time for her shots."

Robby laughed gleefully. "If I could be anyone in the universe, I'd be somebody who doesn't have to go to the doctor."

We never heard Sandy talk again. And by the next evening, she was back on her leash and staying there.

Mr. and Mrs. Keith let us take her for walks sometimes. We throw sticks for her and let her chase us. I was going to buy her a ball once, but I decided to buy a book for myself instead.

"Just think, Will, if she'd stayed, we could have talked to her about all the different planets and all the different people living on them," Robby sadly said one day.

"We could talk with this Sandy about one other planet. If only this Sandy could talk," I pointed out.

"She said others like her have decided to stay here. Maybe somewhere on this planet there are cats or cows or canaries who are really aliens in disguise," Robby suggested. "Maybe there are penguins or peacocks or people just like that other Sandy."

"How much you wanna bet they're all going to end up in our yard?"

4
Aliens Know All the Best Places to Eat

Counting the alien who crashed my birthday party, we had had three sightings. Sure things. By that point, there was no denying we had a problem with aliens. Maybe they don't come by my house any more often than they come by . . . say, for example . . . yours. Maybe I just notice them more than other people do. Personally, I find them hard to miss. There's never been a time when I've had to stop and think, ''Now, let me see. Was that the mail carrier or was that an alien?''

Whenever I brought up the subject my mother just

laughed and said they must be coming here because they liked her cooking. Mom thinks she's a great cook. I suppose there must be somebody somewhere in the universe who agrees with her.

Mom likes to make up bags of these things she calls cookies, though my father says science hasn't classified them yet. She always puts in a few extras so that when we take them outside, we can share them with our friends— as if we'd have any friends if we forced them to eat what she feeds us.

"You know beings that have to travel a great deal eat out a lot," she said once when Robby and I happened to be talking about aliens and why they keep bothering us and she happened to be bagging a batch of her latest creations. "I think they come here because they know they can get a good meal."

"How would they know that?" Robby asked. "We can't even get a good meal here."

"I don't care what the life-form, *everybody* talks," Mom insisted happily. "If the truth were known, we'd find that word of my cooking skill is getting around."

The truth is known and word is getting around about Mom's cooking skill, among everyone I know, anyway. I sure hope the folks in Washington don't find out my mother's cookies and bran muffins are what's attracting all these space creatures to our planet. It would be too embarrassing.

Of course, who knows if aliens buzz Washington as

often as they buzz our yard? Does the President eat bran muffins and oatmeal cookies?

At any rate, at our place it's getting so that Robby and I never know what we're going to find when we go out to play or even look outside. One day Robby was just standing by a window in the sun room so he could see what was going on next door, when he shouted, "Hey, look at that! There's another one out there!"

And sure enough, there was.

We went tearing outside in a desperate attempt to keep that little guy from planting his planet's flag in No Mom's Land. They always seem to like the places we play best. No Mom's Land is not a place we want to lose to alien colonists.

"What are you doing here?" Robby demanded.

"My spaceship is under that." The alien pointed to a rock I could have sworn had been there since the Ice Age (though Robby thought it could have moved just a little).

"Gee, that's too bad," I replied kindly.

"It must have been a small spaceship," Robby said.

"It is now."

"Do you have another?" I asked hopefully.

"Not with me."

Robby and I looked at each other. We were old hands at dealing with aliens. "Go get a beanpole from the garden," I sighed.

"You get one."

"I told you first."

"You're bigger," Robby argued. (He *always* argues. It's very difficult to get him to do anything.) "A beanpole is big. You get one."

"I can't get the beanpole. I've got to plan how to move this rock."

After the spaceman got the beanpole, Robby and I went about making a lever.

"Why don't you just lift the rock?" the spaceman asked.

"It's way too heavy. But with a lever, we can lift things we wouldn't be able to lift using just our bodies," I explained.

"It's common knowledge," Robby agreed. "Where are you going to stick that stick?"

"It's not a stick, now it's a lever," I said as I walked around the rock. "A better question is what are we going to use for a fulcrum?"

"The stick is the fulcrum," Robby insisted as I stuck it under the rock and leaned on it just a little.

"The stick is the lever," I said as I pushed down on it just a little bit harder.

"The stick is a beanpole," Robby pointed out.

There was a loud crack.

"The stick is broken," I said as I held up one end of it.

"Broken," the alien repeated.

My mother says I am her little problem solver. Getting a rock off a spaceship isn't a little problem, but I knew I could solve it. After all, I had just read a book on simple machines, and I hadn't had time to forget much of it. I ran around the house to the garage. When I returned, I had a pulley and some rope.

"Will!" Robby gasped. "Dad's going to be mad at you! That's his pulley that his grandfather's uncle got from his friend who was an explorer with . . ."

"When Dad finds out we needed it to move a rock off an alien's spaceship, he'll understand."

"Yeah. You're right."

"Now, we just need to find a way to hang it from that tree up there and then get one end of this rope around the rock . . ."

Robby corrected me. "Under the rock," he said.

"Under the rock," I agreed. "Then we just have to pull on the other end of the rope. We're going to lift that rock by *pulling* down on this rope," I explained to the alien.

He yawned. "Are you really?" he asked.

"Sure. It's much easier to lift something by pulling down than by pulling up."

"Common knowledge," Robby said as he nodded his head wisely. Then his eyes popped and his mouth dropped open as I threw the pulley that my father's grandfather's uncle got from his friend the explorer up in the air. I got it over the tree branch on *the very first try*! It flew right over the branch and came down on the rock that was on top of the alien's spaceship.

"Broken," the alien said.

Robby shrugged. "Oh, well, Dad never used it anyway."

My father says most important things aren't done on

the first try. He says that if everyone gave up the first time something didn't work right, we'd still be living in caves. That would be neat. Still, I really wanted to help this space guy and not just because he was parked in my yard.

He was going to get in big trouble with his folks if he didn't get home when he was supposed to.

So, of course, I came up with another idea.

"Let's get Tommy O."

"Tommy O.!" Robby shouted. "He can move anything!"

"Our mother gets him whenever she has to move a rock," I told the alien. "He lives next door."

"How much longer should this take?" the alien asked.

I had to think about that for a minute. "Well, Tommy's taking his piano lesson now."

"I have to watch 'Yogi Bear' at four-thirty," Robby pointed out.

"Yogi Bear," the alien repeated.

"Okay. So we'll stop for 'Yogi Bear.' Then you'll probably have to set the table."

"It's your turn to set the table!" Robby said just a little too loudly.

"All right, all right. So I'll stop to set the table. Then we might as well wait until after dinner."

"After dinner you have to do your homework. Don't forget that."

"Homework," the alien said as if he wanted to be sure he would remember the word.

"If worse comes to worse," I said, "we'll finish this tomorrow morning."

The alien pointed one finger at the rock, and without a sound or even a flash of light, it was gone. And, sure enough, there was a little spaceship where the rock had been. It started to puff up and stopped when it was about the size of a bicycle.

"Would you care to explain how you did that?" I asked very calmly.

"No. Do you have anything to eat? Muffins or cookies, perhaps?"

"Get him some cookies, Rob."

Robby didn't argue that time, he just ran and got the alien some cookies. He brought a good, big bag full of them, because, shaken though he was by what he had seen, Robby still knew this was his chance to get rid of some of the little suckers.

The alien reached into the bag, took out a cookie, and sniffed it. Then he nibbled at just the very edge of it and said, "Mmmm. So it's true."

When he got into the spaceship, he still had a cookie dangling out of his mouth.

"Well," Robby said after we were by ourselves again, "on television aliens seem so smart. But this guy didn't even know what a lever is. How do you suppose he gets from one planet to another?"

"I don't know," I answered.

5
Santa Is an Alien?

I didn't notice any aliens around before Christmas that year. I didn't really have time to look for them. I was kind of busy looking for Santa Claus.

I had decided there wasn't a Santa, but I wasn't sure. So I read every book ever written on the subject for my age group and below, which was quite a chore, I can tell you. I was afraid someone would write another one so I'd have to keep going. I thought it was very strange that all those books were so different. How could so many different things about one person all be true? It sounded to me as if there wasn't really a Santa to write about, so people just made things up.

But then, why write so much about someone who didn't exist?

What do you think, Will?

Santa is a spirit.

Santa is love.

Sweetheart, I'm so busy right now. Could you ask me again after Christmas?

Those were all things my parents said when we asked them about Santa. Obviously, they didn't know and didn't want to say so.

"I hope there isn't a Santa Claus," Robby said one day.

"Why?" I asked. "What kind of person hopes there isn't a Santa?"

"Use your head, Will. It's not nice to ask anyone but your mom and dad to give you money instead of presents for Christmas. You can't ask Santa for money, so he doesn't give you any. I'd rather just deal with Mom and Dad. I know how to handle them."

"Use *your* head, Rob. If there's a Santa, who needs money? You just ask him to bring you whatever you want."

"I want money."

I sighed. "I don't know what I want."

"Well, then, it doesn't matter whether or not there's a Santa, does it?"

It shouldn't have mattered. I always like Christmas because in November and December my parents rehearse like mad for recitals and all kinds of special programs and events. In December, other members of Mom and Dad's guitar quartet are always calling or dropping by to practice, there are performances we are allowed to attend, there are performances we aren't allowed to attend, there are all kinds of baby-sitters in the house. "This little house is humming," Dad often says when he comes in from the store at night during the Christmas season. Houses can't hum, of course, but I know what he means. Excitement, confusion, happiness—those things can all *seem* like noise.

Dad's work hours are strange in December because the music store is open more. What with Dad's work and the rehearsals and performances, dinner can end up being any time between four in the afternoon and eight at night. Mom, Rob, and I put up the Christmas tree by ourselves, but we do a little trimming every night after Dad gets home. Mom gives us a time limit. We have to be done in five days. We can do a pretty good job in that amount of time.

When we're done with the tree, it's time to start wrapping all the weird little music pins and tie tacks my mother buys for her students. We wrap the fruitcakes she makes for the people at Dad's store, too, but we know he throws them away on his way to work and gets them something at the bakery. And then the week before Christmas my mother's private students start bringing her gifts. Every night after dinner Robby and I hunt through the living room for the bags and plates of cookies and candy that Mom put down and forgot about.

And then there's our class parties and school concerts and relatives arriving . . . Well, each year, at some point during the last week before Christmas, Mom grabs her head and starts going, "This place is a madhouse! a *madhouse*, I tell you!"

It doesn't get much better than that.

No, the Santa Thing just shouldn't have mattered.

But it did.

"How come I can't find the North Pole on my globe?" Robby asked one night at dinner.

Mom was all dressed up because she was going to perform somewhere that night while Dad stayed home with us. She was feeling pretty good because Dad was going to have to do the dishes and make sure we did our homework while she was gone. Nothing spoils a good mood quite like a Santa question, and just as soon as Robby finished his she looked up at the ceiling and shook her head.

"Well," she said, "I never took geography so I can't answer that one." She turned to my father.

"I have trouble finding Australia on globes," Dad said uncomfortably. "But I'll tell you what. After your mother leaves, I'll play 'Santa Claus Is Coming to Town' for you."

Mom gave us a big smile. "There's something to look forward to, guys."

Actually, it's nowhere near as bad as it sounds. By the

time Dad's through with "Santa Claus Is Coming to Town" (or "S. Claus on the Town," as he likes to call it), it really doesn't sound goofy at all.

"That doesn't have anything to do with the North Pole and the globe," Robby pointed out.

"Our little boy is growing up, Regina," Dad said. He tried to sound sad, but I think he looked as if he couldn't wait.

"You know what I think Santa is?" I said after Mom left. "I think he's like the Loch Ness Monster or the Abominable Snowman. He's an Unsolved Mystery."

Dad said that was an excellent theory, but Robby was determined to prove Santa didn't exist so he could hit up our folks for Christmas cash.

"Then how come no one has ever been able to get a picture of Santa the way people have taken pictures of those other things?" he asked. "How come no one has ever found Santa footprints or . . ."

"Or Santa droppings?" Dad asked.

"Dad!"

Robby and I were both pretty grossed out. That's the kind of thing you expect a kid on the bus to say. You shouldn't have to hear it from your father at the dinner table.

"I am *so* sorry," Dad exclaimed. "I can't believe I said that. Don't tell your mother. But don't you lie to her, either. If she asks you, 'Did your father say "Santa droppings" at the dinner table?' you tell her the truth. But if she doesn't ask, don't mention it, okay?"

"Why would she ever ask us that?" I howled. Robby was laughing so hard that he spilled his milk onto his plate. That was lucky for him, because he'd eaten his bread and butter and there was nothing left there he wanted.

Well, Dad did the dishes and yelled at us about our homework. Then he sat under the Christmas tree and played "S. Claus on the Town" a couple of times and even showed me how to do a few bars. That's when I got my idea.

"I'm going to take a picture of Santa Claus," I told Robby and Dad.

"What for?" Robby asked.

"So I'll know he's real."

"If you saw him, you'd know he was real. You wouldn't need a picture."

"I want to see him, and I want a picture, too."

"You're not going to see him or get a picture, because there is no Santa Claus. Right, Dad?"

I wondered how much money Robby was planning to ask for.

"Santa doesn't like to have his picture taken, Will. It's rude to take pictures of people who aren't willing to pose."

"No offense, Dad, but you were talking about Santa droppings at the dinner table. Maybe you're not the best judge of rudeness."

Dad groaned. I don't know if he was embarrassed about what he'd said at dinner or just having trouble getting out from under the Christmas tree. It had been kind of a tight squeeze for him.

"So can I do it?" I asked.

"Do what?"

"Take Santa's picture?"

"I don't know. I guess it's up to Santa."

"You know what we could do?" Robby suggested. "We could get one of those hidden cameras they have at banks and point it at the fireplace so that we get pictures of everybody who comes down the chimney."

Dad looked over his shoulder at us. "Just how many people are you expecting to come in through there?"

"I'm not expecting anybody," Robby said quickly, "because there is no Santa, right, Dad? But it would be fun to have a hidden camera in the living room, wouldn't it?"

Dad said we didn't have a hidden camera, and when Robby asked him to buy one, he said no. I have noticed over the years that Dad is a lot better at thinking of reasons for not doing things than he is at thinking of reasons for doing them.

I heard Mom come home after her performance. Mom never goes right to bed after she performs. She can't. If she played well, she's too excited to sleep. If she played badly, she's too upset. It's what Dad calls a classic no-win situation. No matter what happens, after Mom gets home she plays the guitar some more or she reads. Sometimes she mends or irons. She's the only mother I know who irons clothes, but she only does it in the middle of the night.

Anyway, I waited until I heard Dad go to bed. Then I got up and ran down the hall to the living room.

"What are you doing up?" Mom asked.

"I've been waiting for you."

"Oh, Will, it's almost eleven. You should be asleep."

"Well, I'm not. Mom, can we buy a hidden camera for the living room?"

"No!"

"Robby and I need one."

"No."

"We have to have one, Mom, so we . . ."

"No, no, no."

I could tell this was going to take a while.

I sat down on the couch next to her. "We need it so Robby and I can get pictures of Santa coming through the fireplace Christmas Eve."

"Of course! That makes sense."

"So we *can* get one!"

"No."

I had made a floor plan of the living room. I showed her where the Christmas tree, fireplace, television, couch, and coffee table were and where the hidden camera would go.

"That is really nice, Will," she said.

"Then you'll get us a hidden camera?"

"No."

I knew I could wear her down, and finally I did. She offered to let me use her 35-mm camera on Christmas Eve. ''If Santa wakes you up, you can come out to the living room and take his picture.''

''Can I sleep in the living room?''

''No.''

It took a while longer, but we finally agreed that I could make a tent out of the dining room table and sleep under it Christmas Eve. Mom's 35-mm camera isn't great, but it beats my Instamatic.

I felt a little better because I had this lousy plan. Still, the Santa Thing kept bothering me and the holidays just didn't seem as good as they usually did.

On Christmas Eve, Robby announced that he was going to sleep in my table tent with me. I said no. He threw a fit. My father said either we both slept under the table or we both slept in our rooms. So we pitched our tent and put our sleeping bags in it. Then we practiced taking pictures of each other in the fireplace, which left us with only three pictures left on the film. That set my mother off, because the film was almost new and she'd planned to use it for Christmas pictures.

''I'm going to bed early. Merry Christmas,'' she snapped.

''I don't think she means that,'' Robby told me.

Finally, finally, we were all in bed. Robby, of course, almost ruined everything because he wanted to get up and watch television while our parents were in their room.

"Santa will never come if the television's on," I told him.

"Santa will never come anyway. It is so embarrassing to have an *older* brother who still believes in Santa Claus. All my friends laugh at me."

"You tell them?" What a thing to hear on Christmas Eve. "Well, if we get a picture of Santa, they won't be laughing."

Robby perked up. "You know, if we get a picture of Santa, we'll be famous, like the guy who got the picture of Bigfoot!"

"Yeah," I said. "The picture will be in a lot of books and newspapers. Maybe even on television. Maybe somebody like Mr. Rogers or Oprah will do a special on the search for Santa Claus."

We both agreed that would be really, really cool.

Robby says I went to sleep, but I didn't. He also says he didn't go to sleep, but he did. At any rate, we both woke up when we heard the glass door on the fireplace break.

"He's here," I whispered.

"Burglars!" Robby hissed.

"It's only Santa Claus," I explained.

"Santa doesn't break things," Robby said, as he scrambled to his hands and knees.

Oh, nuts, I thought. Then I cheered up. At the very least, I'd get a picture of a robber.

I got out of my sleeping bag, found the camera, dug my way out of the tent, and crawled along the dining room rug until I got to the entrance to the living room. I dropped down onto my stomach and watched a little round man dressed all in red and white with two bags from which he kept pulling presents. He had a long list he would look at, then he'd scratch his head and mutter to himself.

"Will, do you see that?" Robby asked.

I nodded my head. "We should have known," I said. "I never even gave it a thought. Santa is . . ."

". . . an alien!"

Robby nearly shrieked the word, and the little man whirled around and stared at us. "Don't you call me Santa," he cried. "I don't want to be mistaken for that old fool."

"You're not Santa?" I asked. That meant I'd just wasted another picture. "Then who are you?"

"I am a highly-trained legal enforcer on my way to investigate corruption among the administrators of the Thalkrid Colonies. But don't tell anyone I said so. I'm not supposed to be here." He looked back at the list. "Let's see, 'Hairy Barbie,' 'High Heels Barbie,' 'Hi-Tech Barbie,' . . . 'baseball glove' . . ."

Robby and I got up and walked slowly into the room. "What are you doing here?" I asked.

"Wasting my valuable time. Hey, do you like dinosaur models?"

"I do," Robby answered.

"Good." The alien pulled two boxes out of his bag and threw them under the Christmas tree.

I didn't want to bother the guy, but there were some things I wanted to know and he was in my living room and all. "Do . . . aliens come here every year to deliver Christmas presents?"

"None that I know of. And believe me, I'm going to tell everyone I know to stay well away from this planet on . . . what do you people call this date? December twenty-fourth? This shouldn't happen to a phlemotle."

"What? What happened? Why are you here?"

The alien stopped what he was doing—which wasn't much—and pointed what we could call his finger at me while he told us his story.

"I was up in Interstellar Space. I was well within Interstellar Space. I was following every regulation of every treaty. Now, not every traveler does that. But I'm in a legal field, and I feel a responsibility to the law. So I know, I *know*, I was where I was supposed to be. I get over this planet, and who do I run into but an old guy with a sleigh and seven tiny reindeer. Can you believe it?"

"Santa Claus?" Robby and I exclaimed.

"The one and only. Guess what he had for a directional indicator? A reindeer with a red nose! Nobody, nobody is going to believe this!"

"Quiet out there!"

The alien stopped laughing. "What was that?" he whispered.

"My mother," I told him. "Why are you here instead of Santa?"

"Because Santa knows a good thing when he stumbles upon it. I only winged the guy . . ."

"You hit Santa?" Robby gasped.

"I clipped his sleigh with my ship. Fortunately for him, I operate with more than a red-nosed reindeer on my craft. I saw him in time and was able to avoid him. Well, most of him. Then I stopped and hailed him and made sure he was all right. And he was. Which was when he got a load of what I'm cruising in. You should have seen his eyes. My vehicle makes his look like . . . well, like a sleigh and seven tiny reindeer."

The alien shook his head. "So then he started in about how this is the one worst night of the year for him to be involved in an accident, he had so much to do, the whole planet was depending on him, the children would be so disappointed. After going on and on like that for a while, he said, 'Do you have insurance?' "

Now the alien started digging around in one of the bags again. "I know what insurance means. Insurance means I could have been circling this little world of yours for ages. So I said to him, 'Do we really need to fool around with insurance?' He said, 'Maybe not.'

"To make a long story short," the alien continued as he emptied one of his bags onto the floor in front of our fireplace, "Santa cut himself a sweet little deal that meant that I'*d* have to deliver Christmas presents to half your world. He's taking the Florida route and will probably be home early."

The alien looked at his list, looked in the remaining

bag, and looked at me. "I have more than half a bag of stuff for someone named Tommykatiedannypeterandmichael."

"Those are the O. kids. They live next door to us."

"Good." He threw the bag at my feet. "See they get this."

Then he looked at our fireplace and sighed. "You guys got a door somewhere I could use?" he asked.

We let him out through the kitchen door. Then we jumped up and down and laughed and cried, "There is a Santa! There is a Santa!"

"Be quiet out there!" Mom shouted.

6
The Players

*Y*ou guys are going to have to clear out of here for about an hour," Mom announced one afternoon.

It had been half a year since the Christmas sighting. Rob, Tommy, and Brendan had been impressed with the alien picture I took Christmas Eve. Dad said he didn't have a clue what it could be, which wasn't exactly the response I was hoping for. Mom said I'd had my finger over the lens while I took a human's picture, and if I couldn't be more careful I couldn't use her camera again. On top of that, either the guy who had hit Santa was already warning other beings away from our planet or the space diners had found another place to eat because we hadn't seen hide nor hair of an alien for the entire six months. I know some people would have been relieved, but I wasn't.

You can get used to having strange beings pop up here and there, you know.

It was the beginning of another summer vacation when Mom got ready to chase us out of the living room. Robby and I had just turned on the television. There was nothing on we really wanted to see, but we're only allowed to watch TV at certain times. You can be sure we find something to look at even if it's one of those boring educational shows about cooking food no one's ever heard of or building new showers in your bathroom.

"Mom!" I complained. "It's our TV time!"

"I know, guys, and I'm sorry. But *you* know I have to see students at odd times. And this is a really odd time and a really odd student. He's an adult who has been taking lessons with some of the teachers at your father's store."

"An adult?" Robby repeated. "Only kids take music lessons and then only because their parents make them."

"Perhaps," Mom said coldly, "when this man was a boy he wasn't lucky enough to have parents who valued the ability to create beauty through music."

Robby and I looked at each other and rolled our eyes. We'd heard that one before.

Mom frowned at us and continued. "Anyway, now he wants to play a musical instrument, but he can't decide which one he wants to play. So he keeps renting different instruments and taking a lesson or two with different teachers. So far he's tried the flute, the electric keyboard, and the violin. Yesterday he had a saxophone lesson that's supposed to have gone very well. But he still can't make up his mind. So your Dad is sending him to me for an hour."

"Dad knows this is when we watch TV," I pointed out. "He should have had this person come some other time."

"What are you watching, anyway?" Mom asked.

"Ah . . ." I wasn't certain.

"It's real good," Robby insisted.

"It's about boats!" I said suddenly. "Or rafts. That's it—that's what it's about. It's about riding rafts on some big river."

At least, that's what I *thought* it was about.

Mom picked the remote control up off the floor where I'd put it and turned off the TV. "I'm sorry, guys," she said. "But work has to come first."

"I hate your work!" Robby shouted. "I hate not being able to watch TV because your students are here! I hate having to be quiet because you're giving a lesson! This is our house, too! Why don't you get a job like normal mothers and leave us with a baby-sitter so we can do what we want?"

Robby was right, of course. It would be great to have

a baby-sitter who would let us do whatever we want. But, geez, I know better than to say so.

Mom had her hands on her hips, and she had this strange look on her face. She always looks like that just before she grounds one of us or takes away the television for two or three days. She looks as if she's smiling, except you can hardly see her lips because they're pressed together so tightly. It's not a happy smile.

I know Robby would never have admitted it, but he was scared. And he should have been.

However, he was saved by the bell.

"That must be Mr. Armstrong now," Mom said as she headed for the door. "Dad says he always brings his daughter with him. I'd like you to keep her busy while I'm working with her father. She's supposed to be very well behaved."

"Oh, that's going to be fun," Robby snapped.

"I'm glad you think so," Mom snapped back, as she opened the door. "Good afternoon," she said pleasantly to the big, bald man with a guitar case, who stood on our front step. His daughter was standing behind him on our lawn.

They both smiled and nodded at us.

"My sons were just on their way out to play. Would your little girl like to join them?"

The man's eyes popped open, and he said, "A chance to play!" He turned and smiled down at the girl. She looked a whole lot happier than we did. She also looked a lot like her dad, mainly because her hair was so short and she was ready to bust out of her pink-flowered dress and leggings.

Mom introduced us. Her student said that his daughter's name was Miss Armstrong.

"What's your first name?" I asked.

Her father said Miss again, this time a little louder as if maybe I hadn't heard him the first time.

"What are we going to play?" Miss asked eagerly as soon as we were alone on the front lawn. We hadn't planned to play anything just then so we didn't know what to do with her or ourselves, either. Then Robby noticed Tommy and Katie O. standing on the edge of their yard looking for us. So we all ended up in No Mom's Land.

There's a storm drain up in the street between our house and the O.'s. When there's a lot of rain, the drain empties right into No Mom's Land and makes a stream. The stream only lasts a day or so before it just turns to mud, and after a few days of that it disappears altogether. We had rain the day before, so there was a little trickle of water for us to play in.

"What are we going to play?" Miss asked again.

Well, Tommy and I don't actually play anymore. We're too old for that kind of thing. We work on projects. Once, we worked on building an amusement park in No Mom's Land. Another time we built a bicycle trail there. Whenever there's water in No Mom's Land, we work on our dam. Tom and I are damming up that little stream so we can have a lake between our houses.

We offered to let Miss help—we would have let her carry rocks—but she said she just wanted to play. So we went to work and Miss, Katie, and Robby decided what they were going to do. We could hear them talking, but we weren't paying a whole lot of attention to them because building a dam takes a lot of concentration.

"Let's pretend we're on a raft and we're attacked by alligators and I have to save you," Robby suggested.

"I don't want to be the one who's saved," Katie complained. "I want to save you this time."

"But I'm better at saving people than you are," Robby objected.

"My mother says I don't have to be the one who's saved all the time. She says we have to take turns."

"I know!" said Robby. "Miss can be attacked by alligators, and we'll both save her!"

I think that's what they did for a while. Every now and then I could hear Miss saying, "When are we going to play?"

"Let's pretend all three of us are on a raft and there's a big storm and we have to hold on or we'll drown," Katie suggested.

"When are we going to start playing?" Miss asked.

"Let's have a dinosaur come to the river to drink," Robby added.

"A baby dinosaur," Katie said.

"Are we playing yet?"

"The baby dinosaur is lost," Robby continued. "We go

over to help it and then its mother comes and she thinks we're trying to hurt him so she attacks us."

"Okay!" Katie agreed happily.

There was lots of yelling and screaming. It sounded like they were having a really good time. They were even splashing around quite a bit, which was pretty impressive when you consider how little water we had to play in. Miss had stopped asking when they were going to play, so I thought even she must be having a good time.

Then the noises they were making seemed to change. I didn't notice it right off, but the sounds seemed to be farther away. And the kids sounded really excited.

Finally, Tom and I noticed that Katie and Robby were screaming our names. We turned around to see what they were doing, and we started screaming, too.

It wasn't the river that had suddenly appeared in No Mom's Land that got us going. It wasn't that I could no longer see the O.'s house or the road and didn't dare look behind me to see if my home was still there. It wasn't the sight of my brother and Tom's sister clinging to a raft in water that I was willing to bet was way over their heads. None of that stuff really bothered either one of us. No, it was the dinosaur Robby and Kate were playing with that shook us up.

It looked exactly like the sauropod on Robby's school shorts, which means it was blue and had a smile on its face. It moved a whole lot faster than I thought a sauropod would move. It kept grabbing at the poles Katie and Robby were using to try to push their raft away. Then it would shake its head and wiggle its backside like a puppy tearing up something it knows it shouldn't have. It swept Katie right off her feet and into the water that way. We heard Robby offer to save her, but she said, no, no, if he would just leave her alone, she would save herself.

"Come on, Tom," I said. "We've gotta get over there."

Old Tom's a good man in an emergency. He'll go anywhere, and he'll do anything. He doesn't care. He dropped his shovel and started shouting, "Don't worry! We'll save you!"

"I'm not worried!" we heard Katie shouting back to us as we ran along the riverbank. She was back on the raft by that time, so we knew she and Robby were safe for the time being.

"Where's that Miss?" Tommy asked as we screeched to a halt right across the river from the dinosaur and the raft.

"There!" I pointed across the river. "She's lying on the raft. She better not be dead or something. Robby's already in big trouble. If that girl was stepped on by a dinosaur while Robby was playing with her, Mom's not going to let him out even to go to college."

"Hey, Will!" Robby shouted. He was standing on the raft and waving at me. "Look what we found!"

"What's wrong with Miss?" I called.

She lifted up her head and waved at us. Then she propped her chin on her hands and watched Robby and Katie.

Tommy started to pull his sneakers off. "I'm going over there."

I grabbed his shoulder. "You can't swim in this river. There might be a plesiosaur in it. You know—like the one in Loch Ness. Or is that a giant sturgeon?"

"A plesiosaur!" Tom repeated. "A giant sturgeon? In the stream between our houses? There's never even been a tadpole here."

"There's never been a dinosaur here, either," I pointed out. "Anything could happen now."

Tom waded in as far as his knees but came back in a hurry when a head popped out of the water, looked at us, and blinked.

"Robby! Robby!" I screamed. "Be careful! There's a plesiosaur in the water!"

Robby looked around in time to see the plesiosaur leap out of the water and crash back in.

"Look, Katie!" Robby yelled. "Nessie! Will, go get a camera. We have to get a picture of this!"

I was going to leave all this to go in the house and get a camera? In his dreams, maybe.

Well, it was at that point that the ground started to tremble. I've never felt anything like it. I thought we were having an earthquake except earthquakes aren't supposed to start and stop like this did. The earth shook, the water in the river sloshed around, Robby's raft started leaping on the waves, and that dinosaur started looking nervous.

Tommy and I looked at each other.

"Oh, no," he said. "Is this what I think it is?"

"Yes!" I screamed, as I pointed past the river and the raft toward the woods behind them. "Yes! It's the mother dinosaur!"

There, out over the trees, was another, bigger, bluer sauropod head on the end of another, longer sauropod neck. The head was smiling, like the smaller dinosaur. But it was one of those smiles you can hardly see because the lips are pressed together so tightly. It was not a happy smile.

And it was getting closer.

Tommy and I yelled and hollered and screamed for Robby and Katie to get out of there. Finally, they saw us pointing and looked up. Boy, you should have seen them jump for their poles then. They pushed the raft away from the shore. Even Miss scrambled to her feet, grabbed a pole, and went to work.

"They'll never get away, Tom. We've got to save them."

Tommy was trying to get his muddy, wet feet into his sneakers. "You're not going to suggest that we get that big dinosaur's attention and then start running so she'll chase us, are you? Because if you are . . ."

"No. I've got a better idea. We'll blow up our dam. Then the river water will move faster and they'll be able to move with it."

Tom sprang to his feet. "Blow up the dam? Okay!"

All the time we were running back to our dam, I was working on the problem of how to blow it up. If only there were a little shack with some dynamite in it. That would do the trick.

"There, Tom, on the other side of the dam! There's dynamite in that shack! We just have to get to it!"

"How about if we go up these stairs and then run along the top of the dam?" Tom suggested. "We could get to the other side that way."

It was hard getting up there because, remember, the earth shook whenever that big dinosaur took a step. When we got to the top of the dam, we could see that she had reached her baby so she wasn't walking anymore, but she was stamping her feet and roaring. The baby dinosaur threw itself on the ground, cried, and waved its feet in the air.

All that made our dam shiver and shake something awful. We had only a narrow path at the top of it to walk on. Tom almost fell off once, but I saved him. Then I fell down, and Tom saved me. Then he started to slip again, and I saved him again.

We saved each other two or three times each that way.

When we got to the shed, it was locked, but Tom was able to break the handle with a stone. Inside we found all the dynamite a kid could ever want.

"There are no matches. How are we going to light this stuff without matches?" Tom asked.

"I think this is the kind of dynamite you don't need matches for," I said. "I think we can make this dynamite explode just by pulling on this string."

I pulled on the string.

"Then what?" Tom asked.

"Ah . . . well, then I guess we better throw it on the dam."

And we did.

Pieces of dam flew everywhere. And the noise! The noise was so awful we expected someone to call the police, and we would have been glad to see them, too.

Blowing up that dam worked like a charm. Robby and Katie's raft came zipping right down the river. It spun around in circles, it bounced on rocks and waves, it . . .

"They're out of control! We've got to stop them!" I cried.

We ran along the river, picking up sticks and reaching out with them so Robby, Katie, and Miss could grab them and be pulled to shore.

"Stop it, Will! I want to save us!" Robby complained.

They were all three of them on their hands and knees because they couldn't stand up the raft was rocking so. Robby had one arm around Miss, and he was reaching for Katie with the other. I don't know what he thought he was going to do while holding both of them like that. I never got a chance to find out because Katie hit him and said, "Stop it, Robby! I'm saving you this time!"

"You're going to knock us into the water!"

"I am not! I'm going to save us!"

"We gotta stop that raft and pull them in before they kill each other," I said.

"Okay." Tom just jumped into the river—this time with his sneakers on—and grabbed hold of the raft. It stopped so suddenly that it sent Katie, Robby, and Miss flying into the water. So, then, of course, I went in after them.

Robby was closest (and he is my brother, after all), so I grabbed him first.

"What are you doing in here?" he demanded.

"I'm saving you," I explained.

He grabbed hold of me. "No," he said. "I'm saving you."

"You can't save me. You're the one who's drowning."

"Come on, Will! Katie won't let me save her, and I want to save somebody!"

Just then we felt something grab us, and the next thing we knew we were on the shore.

Robby spit out some water and said, "Where's Tommy? Maybe he'll let me save him."

"Not a chance."

Just then Tommy landed in a heap at my feet. Someone had thrown him out of the water. Katie came flying after him.

That left only Miss to be saved, and all four of us wanted to do it. We ran up and down along the shore trying to be the one who would spot her first.

Unfortunately, when she shot out of the water she was wearing a big grin and didn't seem at all in need of being saved. She was also riding a plesiosaur.

Then, suddenly, she was just standing in the dirt in our No Mom's Land wiping her hands on her dress. "That's how we play where I come from."

"And where do you come from?" I asked suspiciously.

"A long way from here."

Robby and I just looked at each other and nodded our heads. "I guess we can probably guess where that is," I said.

Mr. Armstrong called Miss from our front steps and said it was time for them to go. Katie chased her across the lawn. "Do you want to come to my house sometime and play Barbies?" she asked.

Miss said maybe. But when Katie asked her to write down her telephone number so Mrs. O. could call to set a date, Mr. Armstrong said he was sorry, but he hadn't brought anything to write with.

"Is her father going to take lessons from you?" Robby eagerly asked our mother.

"I doubt it," Mom said as she watched the Armstrongs leave. "He's trying out the harmonica tomorrow morning. He says he needs an instrument that's easy to carry and doesn't take up much space."

Then she looked at us. "What happened to you four? How did you get that wet and muddy in such a small amount of water?"

"It just sort of happened," I explained.

"Boy," Robby sighed, "that girl sure can play."

"So can her father," said Mom.

7
The Intergalactic
Road Show

My mother has never seen an alien.

She *believes* in aliens. She just doesn't believe she's ever *seen* one.

"It would be arrogant," Mom says, "to believe that we are the only form of intelligent life in the universe. It would also be arrogant to believe we're so marvelous that other forms of intelligent life would want to bother with us."

Arrogance is believing you're more important than everyone else, and Mom is very much opposed to it.

It's right up there with eating artificial whipped cream and peeing outdoors as far as Mom's list of things Rob and I aren't supposed to do is concerned. I understand that arrogant is a bad thing to be, but if an alien plops himself down in front of me and starts to talk, how does that make *me* arrogant?

If my mother had been just arrogant enough to believe that her planet was important enough to attract the attention of extraterrestrials, my whole family could have had front-row seats for last year's Perseid showers.

The Perseid meteor showers get their name because the meteors are supposed to look as if they started at a group of stars named Perseus. I don't have a clue where Perseus is. I can't even find the Big Dipper. During a meteor shower I just lie on my back, looking for little streaks of light in the sky—little streaks of light that *most* people think are made by pieces of broken comets entering our atmosphere. Whatever they are, you never know where in the sky they'll appear or when. You have to watch carefully and know what to look for.

My father asked my mother to marry him during the Perseid shower the first summer after they got out of college. He says he was going to do it anyway, he was just waiting for a special occasion. "By special occasion I was thinking in terms of one of us getting a job," Dad explains. "But we were walking along the beach late one night, and we both happened to see the first meteor. We stood there for the better part of an hour staring up at the sky with our mouths open."

"So your father seized the moment and asked me to marry him," Mom told us once when they were telling us this story as they *always* do *every* August.

Dad winked at us and said, "Yeah, seizing the moment—that really impresses the babes."

I don't get it myself. But that's why the Perseid showers are like an anniversary party for my parents. The four of us pack up food—good stuff, too, like buttered popcorn and salty potato chips and brownies made with chocolate instead of carob—and sleeping bags and blankets and head out for someplace good and dark. Then we lie out on a beach or on a mountain somewhere and stare up at the sky. We spend an hour or two there, looking for meteors. Dad gets up and dances a few steps with Mom, and then Mom is allowed to sing one song all the way through once.

Last year, just before the Perseid showers, we were having problems with vandals on our street. Our mailbox was knocked off its post three times and the O.'s was blown up! Lawn furniture kept disappearing and turning up in someone else's yard. A house was broken into, but nothing was stolen except for some cold cereal and milk, which the burglars ate right there in the kitchen. Garbage cans were turned over next to the street almost every week. Some tricycles were stolen. A For Sale sign was moved from one family's house to another, which made for a lot of confusion. The second house wasn't even for sale, but someone saw the sign and made an offer. It was so much money, the family took it and moved. That made the people whose house *was* for sale really mad because they couldn't *give* their place away.

Tommy O. and I started a detective agency to hunt for the people who were doing all this stuff, though it wasn't any secret. It was three teenage boys who lived on another street. Everyone was sure of it, but no one could catch them. They used to walk up and down our road all day long. "Looking for trouble," my mother said.

Robby and I are in trouble all the time. We don't have to walk up and down the street looking for it. '

Anyway, Tommy and I started this detective agency so we could catch these guys doing something bad. It was a hard job, because we're not allowed to leave our yards without telling our mothers where we're going. My mother doesn't think spying on big kids is a good excuse for going anywhere so we couldn't do as much trailing as we really should have. Besides, these guys did most of their dirty work at night, and I can't go outdoors after nine o'clock. Still, there was always a possibility that we would find some clues. So every morning Tom and I would go for a walk and look for damaged mailboxes and torn-up flower beds, then we'd write down stuff about them in our detective notebooks.

One morning Tom and I were on the case (and walking Robby to his friend Adam's house), when we saw the very teenagers we were investigating. It was awfully early, so we figured they had been out all night breaking things, tearing stuff down, scratching parked cars, and doing all those things that vandals like to do.

"I bet they didn't go to bed at all," Tom said. "They haven't even been home. You wait and see."

We dumped Robby at Adam's house and snuck along the bushes that lined the empty lot next door.

"Look," I whispered. "There are four of them now."

That could have been an important discovery. All summer long, there had always been the same three boys. They'd been around so much that everyone knew them. They used to wave to us sometimes. But they had a strange kid with them. He was older than they were and better dressed. And he carried something that looked a lot like a briefcase except that it was on a strap that he threw over his shoulder. We couldn't hear what they were saying, but the teenagers we knew—sort of—shrugged their shoulders and shook their heads and left the fourth guy standing alone next to the road.

He turned his head toward the bushes where Tom and I were hiding. "I'm looking for Regina Denis," he said. "She lives on this street, doesn't she?"

"That's your mother!" Tom gasped.

"Wonderful!" the boy in the street exclaimed. "Where do you live?"

We came out of the bushes, but we didn't get too close. Tommy and I hadn't actually planned to speak to any of the teenagers we'd been investigating, even though we sort of knew them. We always sort of figured we'd collect our evidence and turn it over to the FBI. We never expected a fourth accomplice—and certainly not one who knew my mother's name. Even those of us who aren't allowed to watch PG-13 movies know that strangers who know too much about you are bad news.

Tom and I looked at each other and nodded. We were about to take off up the street when the stranger said, ''Is your mother baking this morning?''

Now, just who would be looking for my mother and wanting to know if she'd been baking?

''There's an alien out in the street looking for something to eat,'' I told my mother as soon as I ran into the house.

''You just finished breakfast,'' Mom complained.

''But he didn't. They like baked stuff. Do you have any cookies?''

''If you want something to eat, take a piece of fruit.''

''But it's not for me,'' I insisted.

All I got out of her was a couple of apples.

''You're not going to want this anyway, right?'' Tom asked just before he took one and bit into it.

The alien sighed. ''I know it's not considered polite here to ask people you don't know to give you things,'' he said, ''but I've come a long way and I'm not going to be here long. How about one of those bran muffins with raisins and nuts?''

Tom made a face and stuck out his tongue.

''Or birthday cake? I'd be happy to settle for a little birthday cake.''

''Will and Tommy! Get over here!'' Mom called.

''Do you have anything in the freezer?'' I asked as I ran toward the front door where my mother was standing.

"Who are you two talking to?" she hissed.

"It's the alien I told you about. He wants a muffin or birthday cake."

Mom pulled us into the house and closed the door. "You know not to talk to strangers! And you know there's been trouble on the street with teenagers this summer! What are you doing talking to a strange teenager?"

"He's not a strange teenager. He's a strange alien," Tommy laughed.

"He was looking for you, Mom."

She locked the door and made us clean my closet.

Adam's mother brought Robby home in time for lunch. Tommy headed back to his place, and Mom cooled off enough to let Robby and me take our lunch out to the rock in No Mom's Land.

"Somebody asking for bran muffins with raisins?" Robby asked, amazed, after I explained what had happened that morning. "Yup. It's gotta be an alien."

"May I join you?" The voice came from the woods, down toward the creek, not the road.

"We were just talking about you," I said as our newest alien appeared from between two trees. "This is my brother," I told him as I pointed to Robby.

"What are you doing out in our woods?" Robby asked.

"Waiting for you. You made it just in time. I have an appointment with a magazine editor in New York in forty-five minutes. I'm going to have to leave soon."

"In New York City? You're really going to have to move

to get to New York City from here in forty-five minutes," I told him.

"You'll have to move to make it in a couple of hours," Robby said.

"Why did you go in the house while we were talking this morning?"

"My mother called me," I explained.

"Ah, yes. And on this world when a mother calls, everyone comes running."

"Well, when *our* mother calls, everyone does."

"If I asked this mother person to share some of her cooking, she would, wouldn't she?"

"She likes to cook for people," Robby said.

"But she thinks you're a teenage vandal," I pointed out.

"Is that good?"

"Well, let's just say she won't be making anything special for you."

The alien sighed. "I'm here on business, anyway. I didn't make a special trip in order to sample her incredible cuisine. I can't help but be a little disappointed, though."

"Mom doesn't make cuisine. She makes cookies, cakes, muffins. She makes pie, but we won't eat it," Robby explained.

"What kind of business are you doing here?" I asked. Sandy had been a scientist and Leo and Fred were warriors of some kind, but for the most part I thought aliens just dropped by to look around, like tourists. I'd never heard of one who was a businessperson. "Are you a traveling salesperson?" I asked.

"I'm in promotion and advertising," he said. He opened that briefcase thing he had with him. It was full of pictures of stars and pages and pages full of big scientific words all typed up real nice. "I do the publicity for a theatrical company. We're on the road a lot—all the time, in fact—and I make sure that at each of our stops we get publicity in the local magazines and newspapers. I've been here the last six months. Our show is closing this week. We'll be back here next year at this same time, so I need to place a few ads with some scientific journals in order to keep people interested."

"What kind of show has stars in it?" Robby asked.

I grabbed a paper that was passing by my nose. " 'Vaporization'? 'Particles'? 'Radiate'? 'Constellation'?" I read out loud.

"What kind of show is about that kind of stuff?" Robby asked in a tone of voice that suggested he already knew it couldn't be anything he was interested in.

"A meteor show," the alien explained, as he put his papers away.

"A me . . . the Perseid showers? You guys do that?" Robby exclaimed.

"Every year for centuries. It's one of the longest-running shows in this part of the galaxy."

"Oh, come on. Nobody can control meteors," I objected.

"They're meteors to you people. To us they're an art form."

I started to ask him how they did it, but Mom interrupted me. I turned around to see her coming across the lawn toward us and calling our names.

"Look, Mom, here's the . . ." I started to say, and she interrupted me again.

"Can I help you with something?" she asked the alien.

Now, if anyone had asked me that and asked it just that way, I would have said, "No, thanks" and been on my way in a hurry. But the alien thought Mom actually meant it.

"Oh, yes," he said, "I would love something to eat. It doesn't have to be anything special. Whatever you have in your kitchen would be most appreciated."

"I'm sorry, but I don't have anything right now. You'd better just leave."

"What about those cupcakes no one likes?" Robby asked. "You could give him all of those."

Mom grabbed Robby's arm and pulled him toward her. Then she signaled to me with her finger and pointed to the ground just in back of her. That meant, of course, that I had been assigned a spot and I'd better get on it.

"This is private property and not a public park. You'd better be going."

"I do have someplace I'm supposed to be," the alien agreed. "If I have time, I'll stop back."

"That's not a good idea," Mom told him.

"No? I'll have to come up with another one, then."

"He just wanted something to eat," Robby complained as we watched our visitor head back into the woods. "You didn't have to talk like that to him."

"Robby, people his age don't just sit down with a couple of strange kids for a chat. He was looking for trouble. We've talked about this before. You have to use better judgment. You can't keep treating strangers like . . ."

"But, Mom," I broke in. "He wasn't a strange *human*. He was a strange *alien*. That's totally different."

"You can't keep treating strangers," Mom began again, "as if they are guests from another planet. It's dangerous for you."

Needless to say, we were stuck in the house for the rest of the day. We weren't allowed outdoors again until well after supper, and then only because it was so hot and only because both my parents were outside on the deck and only because we were playing with the O. kids. My mother believes the four of us are more than a match for anybody.

We played with the hose in Tom's yard until it was time for the littlest O. kids to go to bed. Then Robby went home to get something to eat, and Tommy and I looked at this magazine he has that tells how much baseball cards are worth. It was pretty dark when Tom went in for the night. I went home and got my parents to agree to stay outside a little longer so I could catch a few lightning bugs. If you catch enough of them, they'll be just like a night-light in your room. It's a good thing I don't need a night-light because I've never been able to catch very many.

As I was leaving the house with my bug jar, Robby was leaving with a paper bag. When he saw me he tried to hide the bag and started running. I figured he must have something of mine, so I followed him. He ran around the side of the house to the picnic rock in No Mom's Land.

"Thank . . ." I heard a voice say.

"Shhh," Robby hissed.

"Thank your mother so much," the voice whispered.

"He's back," I sang behind Robby.

Robby swung around toward me and looked guilty. The alien waved the paper bag at me. "Regina Denis sent me some cupcakes. Quite a few, in fact. I think I'll save them for a little party I'm planning."

"She would have sent them," Robby said to me in a low voice. "If she knew he was an alien, she would have given him as many cupcakes as he wanted."

Yeah, I like to think my mother is the kind of person who would give an alien a cupcake or two.

"Guess what, Will?" Robby continued as if he'd just thought of something really exciting. "That theater he was telling us about? The aliens who run it are always looking for life-forms to work for them. They need people to work the lights and do publicity. He says he could get us a job if we want. We could travel all over the galaxy."

"Work in space? Running a meteor shower? That would be great! What do you have to study in school to do that kind of thing?"

"School? What's that?" the alien asked.

"Oh, boy. This sounds better and better!" Robby laughed.

"How do you learn to make a meteor shower?" I wanted to know.

"There's nothing to learn. You just do what everyone else does. Space is a big place. It's not as if you have to be terribly careful with any of these things. You blow up an occasional space probe, but that's no real loss."

"So we can go now?" Robby asked. He couldn't believe it. Neither could I.

"Oh, certainly."

"Well, that's it," Robby said. "I'm going."

"Mom will never let us go," I pointed out.

"You have to ask her?" the alien asked.

"Of course," I replied.

"Maybe not," Robby grumbled.

"Of course we have to ask her, Rob. You just can't leave the planet without asking your mother. She goes nuts if we leave the yard."

"But she'll say no."

"Yeah, so why even bother talking about it. We're not going."

There was a short pause while the alien peeked into his paper bag. Then Robby said, "I'm going."

"Robby! School starts in just a couple of weeks. We can't go on any trips to other planets."

"Oh, you won't be gone that long," the alien said, as he closed the bag and carefully placed it in his briefcase.

I shook my head. "No."

"Are you crazy?" Robby yelped. "We've only been to Disney World once. We never even got a second chance to go there. Do you think someone else is going to offer to take us around the galaxy a second time?"

"Maybe Mom was right about this guy, Rob. Why does he want to take kids around the galaxy anyway?"

"Oh, it makes no difference to me," the alien broke in. "If you want to hitch a ride with me, fine. If you don't, that's okay, too."

"How do you get from one place to another, anyway? Do you have a ship somewhere? How are you going to take anybody off this planet?" I demanded.

"Oh, you don't have to understand how something works to use it. I am an advertising executive, Will, not an engineer."

"Maybe he's not an alien at all, Rob! Maybe, maybe, he's just some kind of bad human who wants . . ."

"Oh, please! No name-calling."

"I'll be back for school?" Rob asked. "Then I'm going."

The alien stood up. His hand disappeared into his side, into what must have been a pocket.

"No, Robby. You can't."

He put his arm around Rob and told him to wave good-bye.

"He can't take you around the galaxy. It can't be done."

Robby smiled and waved.

"Even if he could, it might not be safe. You're just a kid, Robby, you can't go around the galaxy. You're . . ."

He was gone.

" . . . wearing your bathing suit."

He never heard that last part.

So my brother had disappeared right off the face of the Earth. He was the only person in the world—heck, in the universe—who knew about Mom's cookies, watching meteors, playing with aliens. He was the only person in the universe who knew a lot of things.

Now he was gone, and I was all alone.

And just how, I wondered, does a guy tell his parents that his brother has left the planet?

"Mom!" I cried. "Mommy! Daddy! Come quick!"

I turned around to head for the house and the deck where my parents were reading the paper or doing something equally boring while their youngest son was being kidnapped by an alien life-form, when whom should I meet but . . . Robby.

"What are you doing here?"

"I live here. In the house, anyway, not here in the yard. It is my yard, though, and I . . ."

"But you were supposed to go on some kind of trip around the galaxy."

"I did."

"And you're back already?"

"Sure."

"Shoot. If I'd known that, I would have gone, too."

"We went everywhere, Will. You can't believe all the aliens I've seen."

"I should have gone, I should have gone," I kept repeating.

I could hear my parents running off the deck and across the lawn. I could tell from the way they were calling our names that they were scared.

"Mom! Dad! Robby went to another planet, and I didn't get to go!" I told them. "I'm the oldest! It should have been me!"

"Mom, Will's tattling again."

Mom and Dad just stood there looking at us and looking mad.

"Well, aren't you going to do something?" I shouted. "He left the planet!"

"No . . . more . . . aliens," Mom growled.

"Now look what you've done!" Robby yelled at me.

"It's your fault! I told you not to go!"

"You heard your mother!" Dad shouted. "There's not going to be any more alien talk in this house."

"What about out in the yard? Can we talk about it out in the yard?" Robby asked. He's always asking things like that.

"Do not test me, Robert."

That didn't really answer the question, but it was all Dad said before he told us to get into the house.

I got all cleaned up and put my pajamas on so I wouldn't wreck my bed when I threw myself on it and buried my face in my pillow. "Why didn't I go?" I kept asking it.

Robby snuck into my room and tried to put his arms around me. I let him. "I missed you, Will," he said.

"Is that why you came back?"

"Not really."

He seemed sort of embarrassed.

"It was the bathing suit, right? You were dressed wrong. No? No bathrooms? Didn't they have bathrooms?"

"No, no, that wasn't it. I wanted one of those jobs like that alien's where you just go around to different planets making sure there are stories about the Perseid showers in all the papers. And, well, you know I'm only going to be in third grade this year. They said I couldn't read and write well enough to work for them. They said I have to be older. That alien we saw today is a lot older than he looks. A lot."

"I should have gone. I read above grade level."

Robby said he'd told the aliens about that.

"And?" I asked eagerly. "What did they say?"

"They were really interested in you until they found out you're only going to be in the fifth grade this fall. They said that if you're still reading above grade level when you're twenty-one to get in touch."

"And just how am I supposed to do that?"

"Oh, and I found out something that's really going to upset Mom."

"So what else is new?"

"Tonight is the best night for watching the meteor shower."

"Dad says it's tomorrow night."

"Trust me on this one, Will. We should have gone out tonight."

"Oh, geez. When was the last time something good happened to me?" I asked. It was another question that didn't get answered.

We took our quilts and snuck out through the kitchen to the deck. We could hear Mom in the living room singing along to a commercial. We made it outside without being noticed and peeked in through a back window. Dad had Mom in his arms. They swayed back and forth a few times, and then he twirled her around as if he just might know what he was doing. We laughed and looked up at the sky.

There we saw the biggest and best meteor we'd ever seen. It came from nowhere, and it disappeared into nowhere. But in between it was spectacular.

8
No More Aliens?

"No . . . more . . . aliens," was what my mother had said.

You can't change the way things are just by saying you want them to be some other way. You can't make the weather good by saying it's a nice day when it isn't or become a good student just by saying you are when you're not.

And you can't make aliens into pretend things, sort of like characters in stories, just because your parents say you have to.

When I explained this to my mother, her response was, "Find something else to do with yourselves."

Easier said than done, Mom.

We had *plenty* to do with ourselves. We spent the last couple of weeks before school started shopping for new shoes and working on tree houses. We had lots of human friends who knew how to play all the games we liked. September came, and I had my first man teacher. He brought us Popsicles for the first day of school, which I think more teachers should do for their students.

Having something to do wasn't the issue. The issue was that pretending there are no aliens is a lot harder than it sounds. And hard work is *extremely* tiring.

When you're trying to pretend that something doesn't exist, you have to be careful about where you look. All the time. You can't look at anything too long or too carefully. If you're actually going to *believe* something doesn't exist, you want to make darn sure you never see it. And you want to be particularly sure it never talks to you. You have to be on your toes all the time to make sure that you don't see or hear what's actually there. It's hard work not ever *really* looking at things, not ever really listening.

I found that staring straight ahead as much as possible cut down a lot on the amount of things I could see at any one time. If I opened my eyes really wide and didn't blink, my vision got kind of blurry, which was helpful, too. Robby suggested humming so we wouldn't hear anything we shouldn't. He hummed theme songs from television shows, and I just hummed like a machine.

This behavior didn't win us any prizes with our new teachers; we did, however, accomplish our mission. There were no alien contacts for two months after Mom gave us her order, but we were paying a terrible price. We had no energy left for minor things like homework or music lessons. And as far as cleaning our rooms was concerned? Forget it. We were turning into zombies. I was so exhausted at night I actually *asked* to go to bed. And Robby started falling asleep with his clothes on.

Never once did an alien encounter tire us out like that. We used to complain a lot about the aliens, but they gave us something to think about. Actually, they were kind of exciting. It wasn't hard living with them at all—at least, not compared with living without them.

By the time the leaves were starting to fall, the school nurse had already sent two notes home about how tired and run down we looked. She wanted to know if there was anything going on at home that she should know about. I could have told her. Mom, however, just made us go to bed earlier and started buying orange juice by the drum.

"Maybe it's the oatmeal biscuits and homemade apple butter that's making us weak, Mom," I suggested one morning. I was sitting on a stool with my head on the kitchen counter. Robby hadn't even managed to get that far. He was still in his room lying on the floor next to his bed. "The kids who eat cheese curls have plenty of energy."

"There's an interesting theory," Mom said as she hid some ground-up carrots in Robby's peanut butter sandwich.

"It makes sense. Aliens like your cooking, so it probably isn't good for humans."

Oh-oh. The last time I'd mentioned aliens to my mother I'd been sent to my room for forty minutes. I know exactly how long it was because she had set the timer. That had been right before school started. It had been a while since I'd slipped up. I tried to do some quick thinking to get myself out of the trouble I could see coming my way, but I was just too tired.

Mom didn't say anything for a while. She just kept chopping and bagging all kinds of food we don't like and putting it in our lunch boxes.

Finally she said, "That was funny, Will, that business about aliens liking my food. Do you know what was funny about it?"

Well, no, I didn't.

"It was funny because there are no aliens here. So the idea of strange creatures who've never been here being the only ones to like something is funny because what that means is that nobody likes it. You see?"

"You think it's funny that nobody likes your cooking?"

"Plenty of people like my cooking, Will."

"Sure. But they're all from other planets."

Mom banged the counter with her hand and turned around real fast so she could look at me. I figured I was off to my room for certain. Well, I thought, maybe I'll be able to eat breakfast in bed. But, no, instead of sending me away with a bowl of cold cereal, Mom came across the kitchen and took my face between her hands. She looked down at me and said, "Pretending stops being fun when you don't know you're pretending. Reality is fun, too, sweetheart."

"Golly, Mom, I know that."

She sighed. "I have to go out today. I'll stop and buy the rope you guys wanted and help you make better ladders for your tree houses this afternoon."

I knew that one of my friends was planning to invite me over to play computer games that afternoon, but that sure wasn't the time to bring it up. And I *did* need a rope ladder for my tree house. So I agreed to let Mom help make one for me after school. Then I forced down a huge glass of orange juice that I knew wasn't going to make me look any healthier.

We got off the bus that afternoon and kicked our way through the dry leaves on our front lawn. Mom had left the front door open and called to say she was down in the cellar working on our ladders. She told us to go on out back and wait for her.

"I need something to eat," Robby shouted down the cellar stairs.

"Just go out to your tree houses," Mom yelled back.

"But we're hungry," I explained.

"Would you just go out to your tree houses and see what's out there," Mom ordered.

Well, that was kind of an interesting idea. Usually there isn't anything out in my tree house.

We have separate tree houses that we actually made ourselves with wood left over from some work Dad had done in the store. We each have a little platform with rope walls so we won't fall out. Robby's is right next to the lawn, and mine is a little farther back in the woods. Robby's tree house had a few broken boards for steps. I used a little ladder to get up into mine. They're neat places even if they are so small that our friends can't get up there with us. Sometimes a guy needs a place to go when somebody's chasing him.

That's why we wanted rope ladders. You climb up the ladder and then (and this is the point) you pull the ladder up after you.

A tree house without a rope ladder is just a tree house; with a rope ladder, it's prime real estate.

We dumped our school stuff (the tree houses are definitely too little for homework) and climbed up expecting maybe some butterless popcorn, which is what we get for special treats. Robby started shouting like mad as soon as he reached his platform. I *was* mad when I reached mine.

There was nothing in my tree house, but Robby had a package of those cupcakes that look like pink or white snowballs. They're chocolate inside, then they have marshmallow on the outside, and on top of that they have coconut. I have always wanted one of those. Actually, I've wanted two—a whole package.

"They're for both of us," I screamed, as I jumped down from my tree house and headed for Robby's. "There are two, we're supposed to share."

"They're in my tree house. They must be for me."

"She wouldn't give you two snowballs and me none. There are two in a package and two of us."

"Go look again, Will. I *know* these are for me."

That was exactly the kind of thing Robby would "know."

"Oh, come on, you two. I'm not going to buy you special things if you're going to fight over them." Mom was coming across the lawn with a rope ladder, and she sounded as if maybe making it had not gone very well.

"He's hogging all the snowballs, Mom," I explained.

"You have your own."

"No, I don't. There's nothing in my tree house."

"There has to be. I put it there."

Mom dropped the ladder on the ground next to Rob's tree house and walked with me to mine. "It was right here," she said as she patted a spot on the platform.

"Maybe a squirrel took it," Robby said. His mouth was packed with snowball.

A plastic wrapper floated down in front of us and landed on the floor of my tree house. It was followed by half of one of my snowballs, which made the trip a whole lot faster. Mom and I looked up.

Mom gasped, and I was real careful to look somewhere else.

"What's the matter?" Robby shouted from his tree house.

"Giant squirrel," I told him. "Maybe it has rabies."

"That's no squirrel," Mom said, as she grabbed me and made me stand behind her.

"How do you know?" I asked her. "Have you ever seen a rabid squirrel before?"

"It doesn't have a tail," Mom pointed out. "It doesn't have fur."

A voice from up in the tree floated down to us, sort of like that cupcake wrapper. "Not what you would call fur," it said. "But, actually, we are covered with very fine hair."

"It speaks," Mom whispered.

I heard Robby jump out of his tree house and come running over to us. "We told you so," he said.

"Stop that!" Mom snapped at him.

"Stop what?" Robby asked.

It was clear to me Mom wanted him to stop before he told her she was looking at an alien. Though why she had to be told was beyond me. Anybody could tell what that thing up in my tree was. There was no mystery there.

"Stop talking about it," I told Rob.

"Stop talking about what?"

I nodded toward the alien. "We're supposed to pretend it's not there."

"But why? She sees it."

"You're being rude," Mom said. She sounded the way she sounds when she says things to us like, "Chew with your mouth shut" or "Wash your hands" or "Go to the bathroom before we get in the car." Those are things she says all the time so she can say them automatically while she's really thinking about something else. That's how she sounded when she said, "You're being rude. You shouldn't address . . . ah, ah . . . living, talking things . . . creatures . . . life-forms, I guess . . . as *it.*"

Robby looked up at the alien. "What do you want us to call you?"

"Oh, *it* is just fine. H*e* and *she* don't really apply."

Mom started to get upset. I'd never seen her like that before. She gets mad a lot but never scared or silly-acting or upset. She stopped looking at the alien and looked down at us. "I'm sorry," she said. "I'm so sorry."

Robby swallowed some more of his snowball. "For what?" he asked.

I knew.

And I didn't care for the way Mom's voice was shaking one little bit. I wanted to put an end to that in a hurry. "It's all right, Mom. A lot of the aliens who come here are really nice, just like a lot of humans are really nice. Everything's going to be fine."

"Everything's going to be fine, Will," she said as if she was the one who'd thought of it. "There's nothing for you guys to worry about."

Robby shrugged. "We're not worried."

"Mom, you've been dealing with aliens for a while now . . ." I began.

"For years," Robby broke in.

". . . without any problems . . ."

Robby corrected me. "Without any *big* problems."

Mom took a deep breath, stood up straighter, and nodded her head. "So things shouldn't be any different now that I know what I'm doing, right? If anything, they should be better. Okay, then, you." Mom looked back up into the tree. "You, up there! What are you doing here?"

"I was in the area, and it was close to mealtime so I thought I'd check this place out. I have to say that I find this establishment somewhat overrated. I was expecting things like bran, wheat germ, maybe a little shredded zucchini. That wasn't shredded zucchini on the outside of that cupcake, was it?"

"Oh, gross. Don't even think about it," I answered, while Robby made barfing noises.

"If you want to wait . . . right there . . . I'll find you something else," Mom offered.

"Oh, gladly. I couldn't even finish that thing you had out here."

I looked longingly at the part of a snowball that had dropped coconut-side-down onto my tree house platform. Mom leaned down and whispered in my ear, "Forget about it."

"But I've wanted those things for the longest time," I pointed out as Mom dragged us back to the house with her. "And it didn't even finish it."

"I'll buy you a box of the stinking things."

"Will is getting a whole box of snowballs?" Robby wailed. "You call that fair?"

"As for you, Robert," Mom said as she held the back door open for us, "you are never to leave this planet again. Do you understand me?"

Well, you can only try to imagine how happy I was right at that minute. I was going to get a whole box of those fantastic-looking snowball cupcakes, and Mom had told Robby he could never leave the planet again.

But she hadn't said a word about me.